COWBOYS & FIRELIGHT

A STARLIGHT SWEET ROMANCE

JACQUELINE WINTERS

Editor: EJ Runyon, Bridge to Story

Copy Editor: Brenda Letendre, Write Girl Editing Services

Cover Design: Victorine Lieske

Proofreading: Michelle Josette, www.mjbookeditor.com

rish

Trish Meadows was stuck in the mud.

Literally. She'd known better than to take her compact front-wheel drive vehicle to Wyoming, but it had seemed impractical to spring for a rental when she already had a perfectly good little car to drive. Once she arrived at the romance writers' retreat where she was headed, she had to hand over her keys for the week anyway.

Those were the rules for the exclusive retreat. Ones she agreed to with her application. Never mind that said application had been submitted by her best friend Mindy without her prior knowledge. The contents—questions and answers alike—were a mystery to Trish. No amount of pleading revealed anything her friend hadn't deemed essential.

"You overthink everything," Mindy answered in response to Trish's pleas. "I'm not letting you over-think this. Just go and have a great time. Write all the words!" Only five writers had been selected for the week-long stay. It was to be held at the Holbrook Ranch in Starlight, Wyoming, and included a personal appointment with a literary agent. "You're one of the lucky five. *The* luckiest, actually."

Trish wished her welcome email had included a note about the state of the driveway. She'd made it 732 of the 732.5 miles from Omaha without incident. And now, all she had to show for her money-saving logic was muddy windows and no cell service.

Shoving open her car door, Trish exhaled and surveyed the situation. Her rear tire was half-submerged in murky brown water. She was stranded on an island of mud, dry land too far away for any easy hop.

"I can figure this out," she mumbled. No way would she let this little incident dampen the week ahead. That's just what Henry would expect. Well, Trish was here to prove Henry wrong.

A little mud couldn't hurt. Trish wriggled out of her flip-flops and snaked the loops through a couple of fingers. Her skinny jeans were plastered on a little too tight for rolling up. The deepest part of the hole she'd steered into seemed to swallow only her rear tire. If she could just stretch far enough forward . . . *I'll hardly get the tops of my feet wet.*

Though she'd never tried yoga, Trish imagined her exit from the car qualified for some such animal-themed pose. Muscles she didn't know she had stretched in agony, and she teetered unsteadily trying to get her balance. But when the wobbling stopped, she stood victorious, jeans un-splatted, and on dry land.

Slipping her flip-flops back on, Trish prepared to trek the last half mile to the ranch, which had to be up ahead, around the wooded bend in the road. But two steps away, Trish froze. The Dinosaur. She couldn't leave her precious laptop in the car for some stranger to come along and steal. They'd been together since her freshman year of college.

"Well, crap."

Tossing her shoes aside to keep them safe on dry land, she wished she'd left the car door open. This would be much easier if she had.

Bending only her upper torso forward, Trish tried to see if she could reach the handle, but a sharp rock dug into her foot. She fought the pain, ignoring the rock as her fingers grazed the handle. Another two inches and she could grasp it.

But of course, her foot slipped. The rock kicked loose from its slimy hold and Trish fell forward. She caught herself on the side of her car. But without anything to grip, her body slid along the door until she plopped into the mud. The jeans she'd been so proud to keep dry were now entirely slathered in muck.

Attempts to push herself back up to her feet only served to sink her palms deeper into the sludge. "Are you kidding me?"

The only positive side to this mess was that the road to the Holbrook Ranch was a private drive. No one had come along to witness such an embarrassing dilemma. With any luck, the other writers had already arrived. Hopefully none of those handsome cowboys advertised on the retreat website would encounter her disaster either.

Anchoring one palm on the top of her front tire, Trish pushed herself up to standing. Her poor car would sport dirty hand prints all week unless the ranch had a personal car wash.

Trish looked longingly at the laptop case in her passenger seat. She hated to leave The Dinosaur behind, but she'd risk theft over death by muddy suffocation any day. Her laptop was her most precious possession. She couldn't risk destroying it if she slipped again and toppled back into the puddle.

"I'll come back for you," she promised through her car window.

There was little point in wearing flip-flops with her feet coated in mud, so Trish didn't bother to put them back on. The private drive was mostly dirt, but her soles managed to find what few rocks were sprinkled in. She couldn't quite tell if the weeds along the edge were soft or prickly and decided not to chance it with a scrape already stinging the bottom of one foot.

Around the bend, an expansive log home with a deep covered porch came into view. Most of the home was a single story, but there appeared to be an upper level set in the middle. Hanging plants with pink flowers dotted the length of the porch.

Trish swallowed. This house looked much too fancy to welcome a mud-covered writer in its driveway. She wondered if there was a hose somewhere behind the three-car garage. She'd rather show up dripping wet and clean than crusted over with drying mud.

She wished Mindy were here. Sure, she'd get a tremendous laugh over the whole mud thing, but her best friend was completely fearless. She'd march up to the front door and knock without hesitation. Trish was only pretending to be fearless in hopes it'd prove to Henry that she was a serious writer. One who could someday make a living following her dream.

They'd been dating for nearly six months, until Henry skipped out on Trish's celebration two weeks ago. He hadn't deemed a party centered around finishing a book worth sacrificing a round of golf with his coworkers. Maybe it was Mindy's gift of an exclusive writers' retreat in romantic Wyoming that gave Trish the courage to break things off with a man she once felt she had a stable future with.

If everything went as planned this week, Trish could prove to Henry that writing a book was a great accomplishment. Thanks to Mindy, Trish had an opportunity here to meet with a prestigious literary agent about that very book. If she could make Henry a little jealous with a few innocent pictures taken with some handsome cowboys in the process, well, all the better.

"Here goes nothing," Trish mumbled.

~

WADE

THERE WERE plenty of things Wade Holbrook would rather be doing than hanging curtains. But here he was with lilac patterned fabric draped over his shoulder and a cast-iron curtain rod balanced in his hand.

"A little to the left," Grams directed, light dancing in her eyes at the nearly finished guest room. That smile. It was the only reason Wade was cooped up inside, doing what his very pregnant sister couldn't. "There."

Wade lowered the curtain rod and, using a pencil, marked the spot to drill the wall anchors into place. Grams went almost a year after losing her husband before she smiled again, and as ridiculous as this whole retreat scheme was to Wade, he wouldn't kill that smile of hers for every last acre in Wyoming.

"These are just beautiful, don't you think?" Wade's German shepherd, Shadow, wagged her fluffy tail in agreement.

"Yep." Wade couldn't care less about the curtains, or how cozy this room was for the unwanted guest. It was one thing to host a retreat using the extra cabins on the property, but it was certainly another to host one of the writers in their home. All Wade needed was some annoying scribbler following him around like a lost puppy. But Grams had been most excited at the prospect of offering one lucky writer a personal cowboy chaperone for the week.

"I wish we had enough time to have Kate take some photos of this room." Grams fidgeted with a framed painting of the Bighorn mountains, straightening it.

Wade patted her shoulder. "She's not climbing those stairs, Grams."

"You're right," she agreed. "And I suspect our guests will be arriving soon."

Wade's cue to hurry. Grams had wrangled him into some meet and greet around the fire pit tonight, but until then he'd be out on the ranch. Safely away from all romance writers. "Anything else to do in here after the curtains?"

"I'll grab a broom and clear that drywall dust," Grams said. "Just make sure you're clean and presentable tonight." She moved around him toward the doorway but stopped halfway through. "And on time."

"Yes, ma'am." After Wade finished hanging the final set of curtains, he stood back, as close to the door as he could get. If he didn't make a quick escape once Grams approved, he might trap himself into meeting some of those writers. He wasn't a fan of being made a spectacle, liked the idea of being ogled by romance authors even less. Hopefully Grams would be satisfied enough after one retreat to never hold another.

"Thank you, Wade." Grams caught him in a hug before he could back into the upstairs hallway. "You've no idea how much this means to me."

Tears brimmed her eyes, and Wade squeezed tighter. Losing Grandpa last year had been hard on all of them. They all lived on the ranch, together in the main house: his grandparents, him, Kate until she married two years ago, and an aunt and uncle who were currently in Europe for six months. Their grandparents had raised him and Kate from a young age after their parents passed. The amount of grief he endured at the loss was nothing compared to the grief he'd watched Grams suffer at losing the love of her life.

Lately, Wade had sworn never to let anyone close enough to cause that kind of pain. Better off alone, on what would someday officially be *his* ranch, along with a couple of cousins. Wade was the foreman and ran operations now that his uncle was away, but Grams still held the ownership.

"You going to be okay to welcome the guests without me?" He needed to check on the herd in the north pasture. While he was out that way, he also hoped to steal a couple of hours to work on the base camp cabin that overlooked that same pasture.

"The writers will be so disappointed that they won't get to meet you until this evening," Grams said. "But they'll understand." She pushed him toward the hallway, the clicks of Shadow's claws following in her excitement. "Go on, get your work done so you can charm them over s'mores tonight."

Wade hurried down the log staircase that opened into the central living room, Shadow shooting down the stairs in front of him. The guest suite upstairs had once been Kate's sanctuary. But even though she spent some nights out at the ranch with her husband, Ty, deployed now, Kate refused to climb stairs. "I'm due in less than a month," she'd said to Grams a week ago, when the idea of using the downstairs guest room had been thrown around. "Make the writer climb the stars, not the pregnant woman."

"It'll be so nice to have noise here again," Grams said from the top of the stairs, dust pan in hand. "Don't you think so?"

Wade was saved from answering when a knock echoed. Shadow's oversized ears perked.

"I'll get it." He tried not to grumble on his way to the door, certain with that curtain rod task he'd not escaped in the nick of time after all.

Hand on the knob, he inhaled deeply and forced a smile. Grams would smack him upside the head if he greeted her guests with a scowl. "Hello, and welcome—" But all that froze as his mouth fell agape. *What a sight!*

A slender woman stood barefoot on the porch. Flip-flops with some kind of sparkly flower ornament on them dangled from fingers completely caked in mud. Blonde hair that curled around her jawline swished as she raised her lowered head. A raised hand forestalled the obvious. "I'm a mess, I know." It was the sight of a woman covered in mud that caught him off guard. Certainly that and not her soft hazel eyes that lit up at the sight of Shadow shimmying out the crack of the door.

The sound of her voice brought him back to his surroundings, and he stepped out onto the porch and closed the door behind him. Shadow leaned against the visitor's legs, her tongue hanging off to the side and her tail thumping in happiness at having a new friend scratching her behind the ears. Grams would want Wade to be hospitable, but she'd flip if her guest tracked muddy footprints on her freshly polished wood floors. "You okay?"

"Yeah, fine." She shrugged. "Just a little hurt pride."

"What happened?"

"Your driveway tried to swallow my car," she said mostly to Shadow. The dog's big brown eyes looked back at Wade as if in apology for so quickly becoming a traitor under those scratching fingertips.

The graveled driveway into the property wound through clusters of trees. Most of the puddles were insignificant. He'd meant to put up a traffic cone by the one that wasn't. Mud must've filled it worse than he thought from last night's rare early autumn rain. Wade ducked his head. Those curtains distracted him longer than expected.

"Tried to swallow you too from the looks of it."

Her cheeks turned a deep red as her eyes traveled from her muddy hands and jeans to the mess she was tracking onto the porch. "I'm sorry. I can clean this up. I didn't know what—"

"Don't worry about it." Wade could take her through the back door, into the kitchen. "Follow me."

"Are you taking me out back to hose me off?"

A look over his shoulder didn't help him decide whether she was teasing or simply mortified by the whole idea. "There's a bathroom off the kitchen where you can clean up. I can let Grams know you're here. She'll get you settled into your cabin."

"I'm staying at the main house," she said.

"Oh," he replied, suddenly unsure of things. He'd expected some older woman, maybe one with full-grown kids who'd decided to try writing as a retirement venture. Someone who'd certainly pepper him with questions during his chaperone duties. But he hadn't expected someone so . . . young. *So attractive.*

"I'm Wade, by the way. Wade Hol—"

"Wade Holbrook," she cut in. "I know."

"Of course." Kate had made him a spectacle on the website Grams begged her to help build. He, along with a couple of the ranch hands, had been little more than bait dangled for the romance writers. Wade would do best to remember that, no matter how cute any of these writers might look covered in mud.

"You can rinse off in there," he directed with a nod to the door at the left off the back patio. "I'll let Grams know you're here."

"Thank you."

"Where are your keys?"

"Wow, they really weren't kidding when they said we had to hand them over."

Wade raised an eyebrow at that, but let the comment go. Whatever Grams and Kate had cooked up, he'd try staying out of as much as possible. "I was going to pull your car out, actually. Of the mud."

"Oh." She reached into her pockets and came up empty. "I guess I left them in the car."

He'd need help, but he could grab Allen. His main ranch hand—and the second oldest of the three cousins—should be about done feeding the horses and ready to join him in the north pasture. Allen could help with Wade's escape before any more romance writers showed up. "I'll let Grams know you're down here," he said again, because he wasn't sure what else to add.

The bathroom door closed as he turned away. Shadow sat guard. Wade nearly collided with Grams in the kitchen.

"Who was at the door?" she asked, peeking around his shoulder as if he might be hiding something.

"Your houseguest."

"Oh, that'll be Trish. She's the one you'll be chaperoning."

As if Wade needed the reminder. "She, uh, needs a towel or something. I'm going to go pull her car out of the mud."

"You didn't get the cones up." No one else would consider the lightly spoken statement a means of scolding, but Wade knew better. He'd been so eager to dash away after hanging curtain rods that he'd neglected his most important task.

"I'll grab Allen. We'll take care of it." He kissed Grams' cheek and hurried away before she got any ideas about special introductions. If this Trish looked as cute washed up as she did covered in mud, Wade worried he just might be in trouble.

rish

Lina Holbrook was the epitome of a gracious host. Moments after Trish closed the door in Wade's face, his grandmother knocked and offered her clean, soft towels and the cushiest terrycloth robe. "I'm certainly sorry that hole wasn't marked," Lina apologized profusely. "Wade was headed out to do just that, but looks like you beat him to it."

A hot shower had never felt better in Trish's life than it did after her tumble in that mud puddle. Leave it to her to look like a contestant on a wilderness survival show when meeting the dreamiest cowboy she'd ever laid eyes on. *He probably thinks I'm a helpless idiot.*

Wrapped in the warm robe, Trish dropped her cell into an oversized pocket and tiptoed from the bathroom into the seemingly deserted kitchen. If Wade was still lurking, she didn't want to run into him. It would take hours for the color of embarrassment to fade from her cheeks.

Her muddy clothes were wadded up inside one of her towels. The welcome email said nothing about laundry accommodations, but hopefully Trish could beg the favor as she'd only packed one other pair of jeans. That was what she got for letting her best friend help pack.

The caramel colored floor tiles must have been the heated type; Trish felt the warming under her feet. Glancing around at it all, Trish found herself momentarily lost in the room's beauty. The spaciousness of it was inviting with walnut cabinets, flower arrangements sprinkled around, and a display of cookies positioned in the center of a large granite-topped island. Their aroma lured Trish, her stomach rumbling on cue. She'd been so nervous about getting lost on her way to the retreat that she'd not eaten a thing since she left her hotel in Rapid City. At least, that's what she told herself. It had nothing to do with Henry and his smug dismissal of her biggest dream that bungled up her nerves.

When she couldn't stand her stomach's angry growls any longer, Trish swiped a cookie and took a massive bite. Its warm softness melted in her mouth, along with the gooey chocolate chips. Trish moaned in delight.

"Not half bad, huh?"

Trish jumped at the unexpected voice behind her, nearly spitting out her cookie. Luckily she had the sense to cover her mouth before she sprayed crumbs across the kitchen.

Behind her, a woman about her own age, sandy hair pulled back into a ponytail, smiled. "Grams loves to bake." The woman fidgeted with the cookie display. "And now I can sample for two." She patted her belly, and Trish smiled at the perfectly round bump.

"Oh!" A dozen questions whirled around in her mind, but one thing seemed obvious. The advertised cowboy had a wife and a child on the way. Trish felt her cheeks blaze at her misunderstanding. "Congratulations!" Trish added when she realized she'd not said anything to the wide blue eyes studying her.

"Thank you." The woman beamed, light twinkling in her eyes as she reached for a cookie. "We're only a couple of weeks away from meeting him."

Had Wade been wearing a wedding band? If he had, she'd been too consumed with embarrassment to notice.

"I'm Kate, by the way." She took a quick bite, wiping a crumb from the corner of her mouth. "So sorry I didn't lead with that." Kate reached a warm hand across the counter.

"Trish." She shook the extended hand, surprised by the firmness of Kate's grip.

"Oh! You're our in-house guest for the week!"

"Yep." It was all she could get out considering she'd taken another bite of cookie.

"I hope you like your room. I helped Grams set it up. She and Wade did most of the work, though. They don't like me to do things that involve step stools and power tools at this point." Kate chuckled. "But the lilac theme was my idea."

"I haven't had a chance to see it yet. I had a little incident upon arrival." She raised the towel hiding her wadded clothes as evidence. "Lina was going to show me up there once I finished showering."

"She's probably doing some last-minute checks on the cabins. The rest of the writers are due to arrive soon. I can show you your room." Kate pushed herself off the kitchen island. "Or at least point you that way. I'm not too keen on stairs these days. Why don't you leave those muddy clothes?" Kate pointed toward a door behind Trish. "I'll get them washed up for you."

After dropping her clothes in the laundry room, Trish followed Kate, distracted by the gorgeous home. She'd suspected it was big when she first spotted it around the bend. But she'd been too preoccupied with getting cleaned up and avoiding as many cowboys as possible to pay closer attention.

"This house has belonged to Holbrooks since it

was built, over a hundred and twenty years ago. They knew a thing or two about log construction and it's lasted well. Those are chinked, reclaimed timber logs." Kate tapped a wall as they turned the corner. "Aren't they beautiful?"

"Very."

"This is the living room," Kate continued, explaining where different rooms and features were located, as she'd stopped walking ahead. Her hand rested on her round belly. But Trish's attention was stolen by the vaulted ceiling and stone fireplace. The stories she could write while cozied up next to a fire in this room!

"That's an authentic fireplace. Burns real logs. No gas imitation in this house." Kate's eyes sparkled as she talked. "You'll have to forgive me. I stage and photograph houses, and occasionally I put on my realtor hat and sell one. I have a hard time turning it off."

"That sounds so interesting!" An idea for a new character sparked to life, and Trish made a mental note to jot down her newest idea as soon as she had pen and paper. Yes, this writers' retreat would be a good thing for her indeed.

"The ranch itself—" Kate waved a hand toward a sizable bay window. "Well, Wade can show you that. You'll get to take a horseback riding tour with him around the property tomorrow or the day after, I think." A twinkle in Kate's eyes caught Trish's attention. "Make sure you ask him all kinds of questions. The more, the better."

There was something mischievous in that request, but Trish couldn't pin it down. Probably some inside husband-and-wife joke.

"Have you ever ridden a horse?" Kate asked.

"Yes." Trish was happy to reply that she had. Though she'd moved around a lot growing up, she spent a couple of years in a smaller town with its stable only a mile from the city limits. She'd secured a summer job mucking out stalls when she was thirteen and rode her bike to the stable early every morning. She'd preferred it to being cooped up with the other foster kids who didn't seem to like her a whole lot. "I haven't ridden in a few years, but I rode a lot as a kid." When the owner of the stable tried to let her go because he couldn't afford to pay Trish any longer, she bartered to work in exchange for riding lessons.

"Sounds like you'll be just fine." Kate turned Trish around by the shoulder and pointed. "Take those stairs. It's a guest suite up there. Just a single bedroom and a private bath with a standup shower, but it's all yours! Make yourself at home. While you're here, you're family."

Trish climbed the log stairs to the top, a lump in her throat at those words. Surely Kate didn't mean them quite so literally, but they warmed a spot in her heart. She leaned on the banister, looking down into the living room. "Wow. This is all mine?"

Kate reached for a crooked photo on the wall and straightened it. "Grams insisted our VIP guest receive the best accommodation. Perfect writing space up there," Kate called up, her eyes sparkling with pride. "You can mingle when you want, and close the door when you don't."

"Yeah." Trish's feet seemed planted in place.

"Go on," Kate insisted. "Get settled in. Appetizers are on at four-thirty."

Though Trish didn't know what she'd do about dressing for a meal with her suitcase still in her car, she stepped hesitantly in to investigate the room where she'd spend the next week. With luck, she'd have decent cell reception on this upper level.

She was surprised to find her two suitcases and laptop bag leaned against the wall opposite the tidy bed, her car keys set neatly on her nightstand. "The Dinosaur!" She rushed into the room and pulled the heavy laptop from its case and scanned it for damage. When she found nothing outside of the old scratches and chips, she hugged it to her chest.

Her pocket buzzed against her leg. Trish set her laptop down carefully on the bed and pulled her phone from her robe pocket.

"Have you met him yet?"

Trish closed the door behind her. "Hi, Mindy."

"The cowboy. Have you met him yet? That Wade fellow. Tall, dark, handsome type."

Trish plopped down on the bed, letting her head rest against the fluffiest feather pillows she'd ever encountered. "You could say that."

"Oh, no. This isn't one of those online dating disasters, is it? Did he look nothing like his picture?"

"Mindy, I didn't come here to *date* a cowboy. Please tell me that's not the real reason you signed me up for this."

"Of course not. It's a real writers' retreat. Honest."

"Good. I just broke up with Henry like two weeks ago," Trish reminded her. She left out her secret hope that he'd come to his senses. Mindy would quash that fantasy. Not that Trish could blame her with the way things had gone down. The image of Henry rushing out of their apartment building with his golf clubs slung over his shoulder when he was supposed to be accompanying her to her big celebration still stung.

"Is he a jerk? The cowboy?"

Trish's eyes fell on her suitcase. "Actually, no." Trish had been certain any cowboy flaunted on a website for a romance writers' retreat would be a little arrogant. But so far, Wade surprised her. "He pulled my car out of the mud."

At that detail, Mindy demanded to know every-thing. "Start at the beginning. Tell me everything that happened since you arrived." So, cornered, Trish relayed every agonizing detail from getting her car—and herself—stuck in the mud to meeting Wade on the front porch in her muddy clothes.

"I love it!"

"Excuse me?" Trish wondered if Mindy had been listening to a different story. One that didn't reek of humiliation. "I made a fool of myself. He probably thinks I'm a helpless city girl or something."

"You make that sound like a bad thing." Mindy's tone was flat.

"I'm not helpless. Not even a real city girl," Trish finally said. "Just didn't know how to pull my car out by myself."

"You need to write this down!"

"Yeah, I'm sure it'd make a great comedy. Did I mention the part where I met his pregnant wife and she's absolutely wonderful?" Trish followed the lilac pattern of the curtains, admiring how they let in light without allowing the sun to blind her. The room, all in all, was very cozy. It even had a small writing desk.

"I think you have the makings of a great story opener."

"Maybe."

"Are you hiding in your room?" Mindy asked, changing the subject as she so often did. Trish had grown used to these abrupt shifts.

"I just got out of the shower, remember?"

"Well, get dressed and go mingle with the other

writers. Feed off their energy. I didn't gift you this retreat so you could hide in your room the *whole* time. You need to have some new experiences to write about. Plus, there are other cowboys. One of them might be single."

Though Trish had been unable to locate the actual cost of this retreat, she'd told Mindy it must be too much. But her best friend wouldn't hear any of her objections. "You're like a sister to me, Trish," Mindy had said at the party. "And this is a *huge* accomplishment. You deserve this."

Trish dropped her head against a fluffy pillow. "I don't think everyone's here yet." She recalled Wade pointing away from the house, toward a gravel road that snaked around a patch of pine trees. Were the writer cabins around another bend?

"Are you still fidgeting with your story?"

"No," Trish answered. She'd managed to send off its first three chapters to the literary agent last night. "I finished that, remember? We had a little party?" One Henry had blown off to go golfing because he didn't think it was important.

"Either start writing your next book or go mingle. But do *something*."

"Okay, okay!"

"Don't take this for granted. You've practically been dropped into the perfect story setting."

Mindy had a point. The only reason Trish got stuck in the mud in the first place was because she'd been too busy gawking at sights. The gently rolling hills with snow-capped mountains in the distance; the pastures dotted by wildflowers; the vast openness and promise of solitude with a sprinkle of trees whose leaves were starting to turn yellow.

"You're right," she finally admitted to her friend. "This place is perfect."

"Of course I'm right."

Trish wished her best friend had joined her for this retreat week. Mindy was so much more outgoing. She'd make sure Trish took advantage of every exciting opportunity, even if it meant shoving her out of her comfort zone. "Call you later?"

"You better. And Trish?"

"Yes?"

"Maybe steer clear of mud puddles?"

"THERE'S OUR FINAL WRITER NOW," Lina called warmly as Trish entered the dining room to find a gaggle of women at a large table. Some were munching on veggies and some sort of fancy crackers with dip. Lina stood with a smile. "Trish, please come join us so we can get introductions underway."

Upstairs, Trish had intended setting up her laptop and starting on her new story, but minutes after she got off the phone with Mindy, a wave of exhaustion struck. Knowing it might be the only opportunity this week to get in a nap, she decided to take advantage.

"Come, sit by me." An older woman with purple-rimmed glasses pulled out the empty chair beside her and motioned for Trish to sit.

Mingle. I'm supposed to mingle.

Once Trish was seated, Lina clapped her hands together from the head of the table. It didn't look as if she planned to sit. "Dinner will be served in a little over an hour, but I thought it would be fun to introduce ourselves. Tell us where you're from and what kind of romance you enjoy writing. Maybe throw a fun fact in there for good measure."

"I'm Glenda Gibbons," said the woman next to Trish who'd offered her a seat. "I live in Rapid City." After a quick pause, she added, "South Dakota."

A couple women nodded, as if that answered some unspoken question. Trish thought she might mention she'd spent the night there last night, but Glenda continued before she had a chance. "I write mostly historical western romances. Twelve written and published to date. Working on lucky number thirteen this week. And fun fact . . . I'm a new grandma!"

Thirteen? Trish swallowed. Was everyone else here published?

"I'm Marti Swanson." The woman seated on the other side of Glenda tightened her sandy colored ponytail with a pull as she spoke. "From a small town in Illinois. I write women's fiction, but all my books have a romantic element and western flare. I like my women strong, independent." She reached for a carrot from the veggie tray. "Oh, I like to run every day. Usually five or six miles."

Trish felt panic rise. She'd only finished writing one book no one had ever read, and she didn't think there was a single interesting thing about her. It wasn't as though she could brag about a boyfriend she no longer had. She didn't do Pilates or speak a second language.

Two more authors introduced themselves, but Trish found she'd tuned out until it was her turn. With a sheepish smile, she told the women her name. "I drove up from Omaha." She cleared her throat, wishing she'd filled her goblet with water while she was waiting her turn. "I'm a new writer. Just finished my first book a couple of weeks ago, actually."

The table erupted in excitement and words of praise. Trish surveyed the smiling women in suspicion. "It's just one book."

"Finishing your first book is *huge!*" Glenda cooed. "It took me six years to finish my first one. I hope you celebrated?"

The first bits of pride burst from Trish. These women *understood*. "I had a small party," she admitted, deciding to leave out the detail about Henry skipping out. "It was fun."

"Have you started your next?" another author asked—Lizzie, maybe?

"That's what I hope to work on this week," Trish answered.

"What about a fun fact?" Lina asked. "What can you share with us?"

Trish tried to think of something. Anything. But her day job working in a cubicle for a large corporation wasn't something she considered interesting. In fact, only Henry seemed to think she'd landed a golden opportunity to build a career with a prestigious company. "I don't know what there is to tell," she finally admitted. "Writing is my interesting fact."

"Oh, surely there's something," Glenda said. "Any pets?"

"Not even a goldfish."

"Surely a young, pretty thing like you has a special man in her life?" Marti—the one with the ponytail—added.

"Well . . ." Trish debated how much to spill. She hadn't intended to tell anyone about Henry. But these women, with their encouraging smiles and trusting eyes, broke her. "I was dating a man, Henry. He was supposed to come to my book celebration party, but he didn't think it was important. He decided last minute to go golfing instead."

The hisses of disapproval echoed in the room, empowering Trish to continue.

"We'd been dating for six months, but I broke it

off after that," Trish said. "Kind of here to prove him wrong, actually. He can't grasp my dream to write. At least, not without some kind of contract with a publisher."

"Honey, you are so much better off without him!" Marti said.

"I hope you're planning to make that man realize what he had?" Glenda nudged her with her shoulder. "We *do* get to take pictures with some dreamy cowboys tomorrow. Post those puppies online and give him something to be jealous over."

For the first time since she arrived, Trish felt herself completely relax and excitement took over. This week could be exactly what she needed. To be surrounded by positive, likeminded writers and some attractive cowboys perfect for story inspiration—*yes, this week could be good indeed.*

"Speaking of the photoshoot," Lina interjected, "I'd like to cover some itinerary items. Everyone should have found a folder in their room." Lina waved a dark pink portfolio for them to see. "It has the schedule for the week for each of you. We'll try to meet up once a day to talk about your progress or any points you're stuck on in your stories. Some of the events are group events. Other events, like your scheduled session with our agent, are individual."

"When is that?" Marti asked.

"Thursday," Lina answered. "Taylor Voss will be

joining us through Skype. We have a private room set up with a computer and webcam."

Three days from now. It was scary and exciting. Trish couldn't wait. Maybe then, after she had an agent to back up her book, Henry would have to admit that her dream to be an author was legit.

"When do we get to meet the cowboys?" Glenda asked.

"After dinner," Lina answered. "Wade, my oldest grandson, will get a fire going on the back patio so we can make s'mores."

Trish had hoped she'd avoid Wade for at least the rest of this day. Maybe by tomorrow he'd get her confused with one of the other writers or forget about their messy meeting.

Glenda leaned close and in a low tone said, "You're extra lucky. You get that handsome cowboy as your personal escort all week."

Trish took a sip of ice water and mentally reminded herself that he wasn't available. The memory of Wade standing in the doorway, filling out a fitted T-shirt rather well, mouth frozen open in shock, made her heart do a little pitter-patter.

CHAPTER 3

ade

THE LOWERING SUN warned Wade he should soon
head back to the house. Allen had gone home a
couple of hours ago, but he had busied himself with
the new deck for his cabin. Well, he considered it his
cabin anyway. Grams knew he was fixing it up a
little, but she likely had no idea the extent. She didn't
venture out to the north pasture much anymore.

Shadow sat on the spot where Wade would eventually add a railing, her tail swishing lazily. Two eyes
peeked up along the deck's edge, intently fixed on
that tail. Shadow seemed oblivious to the cat about to
pounce.

"Think we should probably head back, huh?" he said to the dog.

Shadow's eyes met his, but she didn't so much as lift her chin at that statement. She liked it out here as much as he did. The north pasture offered the quietest place on the entire ranch. It also offered the best views of the Bighorn mountains and breath-taking sunsets. He often wondered why his great-grandpa built the main house so far south. But a house that size would never fit as well as this one-room cabin did, nestled in these rolling hills.

Before Wade could force himself to stand, the gray-striped cat he'd named Squirrel sprang onto the deck and attacked Shadow's tail. Shadow shot up in surprise, but before she could catch the culprit, the cat shot off the side of the deck.

Wade let out a good laugh at the show but then, out of excuses to stay away, he started up his ATV. "C'mon, girl. We gotta head back."

Shadow sniffed along the edge of the deck for her attacker, but had to admit defeat when Wade gave a sharp whistle. Once she hopped on the back, Wade turned the ATV toward the house. Grams would be livid if he stayed out much later. Time to head back and brave the new guests he'd never admit were unwanted. Animals were so much easier to hang out with than people. Add that those people were writers, extra curious about the cowboy lifestyle, and Wade may as well have volunteered to be on a reality show.

"Writers," he mumbled as he maneuvered through the narrow dirt trails, trying to avoid the bumps for Shadow's sake. "Why writers, Grams?"

Earlier today there'd only been one. Now there'd be five of them. Hopefully no one else had gotten stuck in the mud. He and Allen had snuck back before lunch to fill the hole and set up cones before anyone else arrived. But no doubt he'd hear about his poor timing. Grams would probably insist he wash Trish's car. The number of muddy handprints still made him smirk.

All Wade wanted was a quiet life. One in which he could get up at the crack of dawn and see to the needs of his ranch. His animals. His land. Then come home in the evenings, eat a simple meal, and sit quietly by the fire with a loyal dog and perhaps a cat. In the warmer months, that meant sitting outside around a fire pit. Tonight, Wade was expected to share that fire pit in the company of a bunch of chatty women.

Wade was forced to park his ATV farther away than usual, near a grove of trees. There was a car with an Illinois license plate in his usual space.

"One week," he grumbled under his breath. He could handle one week as long as Grams didn't get it in her head to host more of these retreats.

Through the bay window, he could see into the dining room. The large table, hardly ever used now that so many of their family members were gone, was surrounded by women. Wade scowled for a moment, quite irritated by the disruption of his quiet evening. But then he saw Grams laugh out loud, her smile so wide her eyes were squeezed closed.

He hadn't seen a smile that heartfelt since Grandpa had been gone.

In that moment, the cold shell around Wade's heart softened. Even if he hated every minute of this week, he'd endure it for Grams. His mom, he'd often been told, had died of a broken heart. He didn't want the same fate for the woman who raised him.

Kicking off his dirty boots at the door, he tossed his hat onto a hook and braved the writers' ambush.

Someone gasped. "Is that him?"

Wade wasn't close enough to see Grams' face, but her hands clapped together in excitement. "Wade, you made it!" The smile she wore faded at the sight—and likely, smell—of him.

Wade scanned the gathering, noticing that of the strangers at his table, three likely had kids his age. Maybe even grandkids, though he'd not dare speak that observation out loud. The other woman looked to be about Trish's age, maybe a couple of years older.

"Broken water line in the north pasture. Had to

get it fixed today." Wade felt it unnecessary to mention that he'd handled that problem shortly after lunch. The writers were eating up his words, so maybe Grams wouldn't call him out in front of them. Trish had her eyes turned toward the table, hands fidgeting with a plastic spoon. "There's no water up there otherwise. Not enough to go around anyway. We don't want to give the cattle a reason to seek standing water."

"What if you weren't able to fix the line?" a woman with purple-rimmed glasses asked, pen poised at the ready. It was then that Wade noticed the lack of dinner plates. They'd finished their meal and were picking at bite-sized finger desserts, little cheesecakes and mini cupcakes.

"It was either fix the water problem or move the cattle. Didn't have enough help today to accomplish that quickly," Wade explained. His eyes wanted to land on her, this introverted blonde, which forced him to look at everyone else instead.

"I'd like to formally introduce everyone to my oldest grandson, Wade Holbrook, ranch foreman. He runs the operation here."

"He's so young!" one of the writers cooed to Grams.

"Wade knows the place better than anyone," Grams boasted. "He's worked on the ranch since he was old enough to walk."

When the doting looks were too much to take, he spread his hands wide. "Better get washed up for you ladies."

"Please do," Grams said, a teasing edge to her voice. "Don't want to frighten away our guests on the first night."

"Yes, ma'am." He smiled his dazzling smile for the writers as he promised Grams he'd do a few times during their visit. "Ladies, if you'll excuse me." He nodded at them and could've sworn one made some kind of swooning noise. *Oh, brother.*

Most nights, Wade settled for washing his hands in the kitchen sink, warming a plate of leftovers, and eating at the dimly lit kitchen table with a view of the backyard. That was how life would be one day, once his cabin overlooking the north pasture was finished. Okay, maybe there wouldn't be many leftovers unless he occasionally commandeered some. But frozen dinners and the occasional grilled burger or steak sounded doable. He could live with that.

Wade passed through the kitchen, heading toward the bathroom near the back door. He probably should have snuck in through there and showered first, but he'd wanted Grams not to worry. She did that more often now that Grandpa was gone.

A couple of his cousins who doubled as ranch hands came out to help every day, but today he had been down one. The hot water did its job reviving him, the steam easing the ache of his muscles from a hard day's work.

It was too much to hope that hiding in the shower would make those women disappear, so when his fingers started to wrinkle, Wade dried off.

He slipped on the clean jeans and a worn T-shirt he'd left there this morning, wondering what the romance writers would think of a cowboy who looked an awful lot like an ordinary man.

Wade went in search of leftovers in the dark kitchen. He'd just stuck a plate of pot pie to heat in the microwave oven when he caught sight of a shadow.

From the opposite end of the island, Trish reached toward a plate of cookies.

"Stealing cookies?"

She startled, a tiny little mouse squeak of surprise, and hopped back. "You weren't supposed to see me."

"You haven't answered my question." He tried to ignore how cute she looked with those wide eyes and her reddening cheeks showcased in the glow of the light over the kitchen sink. He doubted she'd ever gotten away with much in life considering how easily the slightest guilty thought showed in her expression.

Her hand hovered above the tray, fingers curled in the cookie-grabbing ready position. "I thought I might get hungry later."

"You have something against s'mores?"

"I love them." She finally swiped a cookie. "And cookies."

"You might have to fight Kate for them," he said. The timer dinged on the microwave and he pushed at the open button. "She's eating Grams' cookies like they're potato chips."

"Kate," Trish repeated, as though the name meant something to her. Wade couldn't read what else was there, but he did notice it was. He wondered if they met before dinner. Kate didn't leave the house much these days if she was still there after dark. He asked, "You met her, I assume?" She hated the bumpy roads, and her belly was having a harder time fitting behind the steering wheel.

"Yes." Trish stuffed two cookies inside a napkin. "Very lovely woman."

Wade laughed at that. "If you say so." Leaving Trish with her puzzled expression, he carried his plate over to the high-top table set against a window. It overlooked the raised flowerbeds between the house and the garage. The setting sun always made the flowers appear as if they were ablaze.

"You any good with starting a fire?" Wade asked after a few bites because Trish hadn't slipped out of the kitchen. Her eyes kept falling to the window near his table.

"I might know a thing or two." She leaned her weight against the counter and munched on a cookie she hadn't stashed for later. "I earned a camping badge in the third grade that says I do."

Wade smirked at that. Witty. "Want to put those skills to good use and help me get the fire pit going after I finish up?"

"Okay."

"Might want to grab a jacket or something. It gets down to the forties this time of year. Even with a fire, you'll probably be chilly."

With a silent nod, Trish slipped out of the kitchen, leaving him in the glow of the setting sun to finish his dinner. But his eyes followed her until she turned a corner and faded away. In a week, she'd fade away for good. The thought caused him to shift in his chair and forced his attention back to his plate.

It'd probably been a mistake to invite Trish to help him get things set up. But it would make Grams happy that he was doing something to include the writer who was supposed to be under his special care. At least he had a few minutes to reinforce his walls.

It wouldn't matter if she was staying. He wasn't about to let any woman steal his heart. Not after watching the agony Grams endured at Grandpa's passing. For weeks, she didn't eat. She didn't sleep. She wandered the house, lost. Anything could make her start sobbing in grief. It still happened, but less frequently now with a year gone by.

Grams was stronger than anyone he knew. It was

the only reason she survived the heart-wrenching grief. Wade wasn't sure he was that strong. He'd best stick to things he knew he could survive. Since a broken heart wasn't one of them, it was imperative that he keep his guard up around the alluring Trish Meadows.

CHAPTER 4

Trish couldn't imagine any reason Wade would invite her to help him set up the fire except that her attendance fee covered her own personal cowboy chaperone for the week. That had to be it. Of course, the itinerary failed to mention that said cowboy chaperone had a very pregnant wife.

She yearned to retrieve her phone and call Mindy. Request rescue via a fake family emergency. Besides the fact Henry would surely laugh in her face if he learned about this disaster and reinforced his belief that her dreams weren't practical, Mindy would never let her leave.

Instead, Trish dug out her Nebraska Huskers

sweatshirt she'd only intended to sleep in and headed outside. Next time, she wouldn't let Mindy help her pack. Most of the clothes that made the trip were impractical for Wyoming in early September.

"You even have room for s'mores after all those cookies?" Wade asked when she stepped from the kitchen and onto the stone terrace. The same fluffy German shepherd from earlier bounded toward her and shoved her body against Trish's legs, demanding attention. Though dusk was settling, she could make out some of the intricate brick pattern of the terrace floor. It was safer to study that than the strong biceps lifting the iron lid from the raised fire pit.

She scratched the dog behind the ears, and that contented thumping tail said she seemed to enjoy it. If her delightful moans were any clue, enjoyed it a lot. "I'll have you know, I haven't had more than that one cookie since this afternoon, when your wife showed me around." There, now it was out in the open. She didn't want him to think there'd been any . . . misconceptions.

"My— Oh, Kate." Wade wore a smirk, but he didn't let on why. "Mind grabbing some twigs we can stick in the bottom? Shadow'll just chew them to pieces."

"On it." Though she'd yet to see Wade with a wedding band, her worst suspicions were confirmed. Well, not for Wade or Kate. She was certain they were quite happy. Who wouldn't be with a baby on the way? But for Trish, it was simply another reminder that her hope to make Henry jealous was pitiful at best.

Maybe she could still get some good writing material from this cowboy. Pepper him with questions, as Kate had insisted. And with a week dedicated to writing, who knew what she might come up with for her *second* book.

Gathering as many loose twigs as she could, she dropped them into the fire pit. Shadow stole one from the pile and sprinted away. The thought of having another completed manuscript brought a giddy smile to her face. Surely *two* books would force Henry to recognize the truth about Trish's passion more than any flirty posts about cowboys ever would.

"Need me to grab some firewood?" Trish nodded toward the covered shelter filled with stacked wood.

"Grab three or four to start?"

Trish maneuvered her way around the cast iron patio chairs and benches covered in floral cushions and set in a circle around the metal fire pit. A stack of blankets threatened to topple on one bench.

A few feet from the wood pile, Trish spun around. "Should I be leery of anything? Snakes? Scorpions? Werewolves?"

Wade stared blankly at her for a moment, and she felt the heat flush to her cheeks. So much for trying to be funny.

"'Fraid we're a little short on werewolves. But

you might want to brace yourself for spiders." He dug into his jacket pocket and pulled out a pair of gloves. "Here, put these on."

She caught them, which was a point of celebration with the growing darkness. They were at least two sizes too big, and Trish caught herself acutely aware of how big his hands must be to fill those gloves. Strong, manly hands.

She shook the thought away. *He's married.*

Trish reached for a split log near the corner. "When's Kate due?" Trish decided the best way to keep that little detail at the front of her mind was to ask about this.

"Sometime next month, I think?"

She reached out toward the second log, and froze mid-reach. "You don't know?"

Wade lifted the lid from the fire pit and set it in the grass nearby. "I'm not great at keeping track of those things."

Turning her attention back to the wood pile, Trish tried to understand how that was possible. Some men just weren't good with dates—birthdays, anniversaries, and she guessed, due dates of their children. It was possible. Not that she had firsthand experience with which to compare. "Do you know what you're having?"

"What who's having?" Lina chimed in, closing the sliding glass door behind her.

"It's a boy," Wade chimed in. "Kate's having a boy."

"Oh, yes. Two weeks away, too! Or at least, that's what the doctors predict. But no Holbrook has ever come when they're supposed to. They have a habit of being early." Lina dropped another stack of blankets on a chair. "Let's hope Eli's father will be here to meet him."

Trish nearly fumbled the three chunks of wood she'd stacked in her arms. Why wouldn't Wade be here for that? She wanted to ask about the comment, but outside of the question seeming far too personal, the sliding glass door to the kitchen slid open. Kate carried a tray filled with goodies—graham crackers, chocolate, and giant marshmallows—to the main table.

"You a s'mores fan?" Kate asked Trish once she'd dropped the logs next to the fire pit. She knew how to light a fire, but she doubted Wade was going to bestow her the privilege.

Backing away a few steps, Trish dropped onto a padded bench. "I love 'em! It's fun to try them different ways. My favorite have strawberry and banana slices."

Wade paused to peer at her over his shoulder in what must be disbelief. "Really?" He'd stopped lighting a folded piece of thin cardboard as if she'd just suggested they try the treat with mustard.

"It's so good." She refused to back down to the

closeminded cowboy. "A neighbor of mine growing up taught me several different s'mores varieties, but my favorites always included fresh fruit."

Kate eyed an empty chair but seemed to decide against sitting when her hand went to her lower back. "You know what? I saw some bananas and strawberries in the kitchen. I'll go slice some up."

Before Trish could tell her not to trouble with all that, Kate zipped inside—quite fast for a very pregnant woman—Lina close on her trail, explaining, "Need to gather up all the writers and find out where our other two cowboys ran off to."

Wade made a noise, and not a pleasant one, once Lina slid the door closed behind her. "Is that what all you city girls like to do? Fancy up stuff when it's not necessary?" Wade asked as the first trace of a flame licked the bottom of the biggest piece of wood. "I don't understand why you would want to ruin a perfectly good, *classic*, s'more."

Trish took a deep breath. "I'm not a city girl." She just happened to live in a city. They were completely different things. "Why don't you knock it *after* you've tried it?"

"No way." Wade stirred the glowing embers with a thin stick until the fire took hold and the threat of it dying faded. "I don't fix what's not broken."

"You mean you don't like trying new things."

"I—"

Wade was cut off when Lina stepped back onto

the patio, a gaggle of women behind her. "Everyone, please find a seat and get cozy. Blankets are over there." Lina pointed to the toppling pile. "I thought an evening around a fire pit would be a great way to kick off our writing retreat week. Give you a feel for Wyoming in the fall."

"I hope the leaves finish changing colors while we're here," Marti said as she wrapped a blanket around her legs and fell into a chair opposite the patio door. "I bet it's just gorgeous when that happens."

Trish hoped they'd be around long enough, too. Wyoming in the fall had to inspire quite the romance novel.

"Is that a bear?" One writer pointed to the fluffy mass sprawled in the grass. The stick she'd stolen was long gone, and now Shadow was rolling in the grass, all four paws in the air.

"That's Wade's dog, Shadow," Lina said. "Don't worry, she's friendly." Lina realigned the stack of napkins and plastic cups. "Our other two cowboys, also grandsons of mine, should be arriving any minute. They keep pretty busy on the ranch, but I've convinced them to join us for a couple of events, like our photoshoot tomorrow."

"Don't suppose they're up for being personal chaperones, too?" Glenda asked with a hearty laugh that made it necessary to readjust her glasses.

Lina patted Wade on the shoulder. "I'm afraid that privilege is reserved for Wade."

Trish suspected Wade had been strong-armed into that *privilege* by the two women who ran the household. Why else would he agree? It was written all over his scowling face—lit by the glow of the fire—he didn't like it one bit.

"Trish, you're a lucky girl," Lizzie hooted. "If you ever get tired of that cowboy, feel free to share!"

"Speaking of cowboys," Kate said, after setting bowls of freshly sliced fruit near the s'mores platter and giving Trish a wink. "I better go round up Allen and Chet. I think I saw them pull up."

"Do they both live with you, Kate and Wade?" Glenda asked Lina once Kate slipped back inside and Wade sauntered off toward the wood pile again. "Out here full-time?"

Trish thought the question was odd. Why would one live out here and not the other?

"Wade does," Lina answered. "Kate's only here off and on until her husband, Ty, returns home from his deployment." Lina continued on, more about where Kate's husband was stationed and what he was doing for the Army, but those details were a blur. A tiny bubble of rage built up in her chest. Wade had *let* her believe that Kate was his wife. He hadn't bothered to correct her earlier though he had a couple of opportunities.

Miffed, Trish bounced around the excuses to slip

away early. She finally settled with a headache. It was as near to truth as she was going to get. As she pushed out of her chair, about to announce an early bedtime to the group, Wade brushed by her carrying another four pieces of split wood. It was bad enough he was smug and closeminded, but did he have to make her breath catch at such minor contact?

"You forgot the task you took on," he whispered, as though she failed some sort of test. "I had to fight the werewolves off myself."

He'd be hilarious if Trish didn't have the urge to shove him toward the now-roaring fire. Darn smug cowboy, letting her make a fool of herself. Maybe tonight she should try writing a murder mystery. "Looks like you came out unscathed. Too bad."

"Our guests of honor have arrived!" Kate announced. "Ladies, meet Allen and Chet."

Two men, both wearing cowboy hats and belt buckles that reflected the fire, stood near the patio door. One had his hands shoved into his pockets as though he wasn't really enjoying the attention, but had probably been forced to attend. The other— Allen, Trish thought—was very charismatic. He waved a guitar toward the group. "I'm the good-looking one. Got my looks from Grams," he said with a wink as he found a seat. The shy cowboy followed behind him and dropped into a chair.

"Now we can get started!"

If it weren't for the flow of excitement in Lina's

eyes, Trish would have excused herself. But something about that genuine smile shoved Trish back into her seat. She could tolerate Wade for another hour if she didn't have to do it alone.

"Wade," Lina called. "Please, sit down."

Wade surveyed the group first, then the chairs. "Looks like this is the last seat," he said to Trish with a nod at her half-empty bench. He waited for her to scoot over before he sat down. Trish hugged the iron armrest to avoid her leg brushing against his, but it was no use. His strong, muscular legs took up most of the bench.

"What does a cowboy *do* exactly?" Lizzie asked.

Allen leaned forward and removed his hat, flashing a smile. "It might be easier to answer what a cowboy *doesn't* do."

"Oh, brother," Trish heard Wade mumble. For some reason, it really amused her. "Here we go." His eyes met Trish's for a brief moment. Long enough for her to see the firelight dance in their reflection. Her heart did a funny fumble.

"You two want some s'mores?" Glenda held out a tray, bumping Trish in the arm with it. "The marshmallows're going fast."

"Thanks." Trish set the tray in her lap and waited for the forked rod to be passed over. "You lied to me," Trish said softly as Allen rambled on about life on a ranch. She should probably be taking notes, but she couldn't pass up the opportunity to confront Wade.

He glanced at her askew. "About what?"

She stuck a marshmallow on both ends of the forked rod and reached it toward the fire. "Your *wife*. Kate."

After a shoulder roll, Wade leaned forward, resting his elbows on his knees. "More of an omission, actually."

"Same difference." Trish turned the rod to even out the golden coloring on the roasting marshmallows.

"She's my sister," Wade finally said. He dug into the packet of graham crackers and snapped two in half. "I'm sorry. I didn't really think about it. I just thought it was better if you believed . . ." He captured her two golden marshmallows between the crackers but didn't finish his sentence.

"Believed what?"

"Nothing."

Wade reached for one of the s'mores, but Trish caught his hand. "I don't think so." Her breath caught at the heat of his touch. It had to be the fire. Hopefully he hadn't noticed her ridiculous reaction.

"I don't get one?"

"Only if you try it my way. Otherwise, I'm giving yours to Shadow." At the mention of her name, Shadow hopped up from her spot in the grass and poked her nose through the armrest of the bench on Wade's side.

"No way. Chocolate's bad for dogs."

"I wouldn't feed chocolate to a dog." Trish narrowed her eyes at him. "You owe me." She carefully constructed one s'more, adding a slice of banana and strawberry on top of the marshmallow. She flipped it over and added the slab of chocolate underneath. "Try this. If you don't like it, you can have the other one."

Wade took a cautious but decent-sized bite and chewed slowly. A string of melted marshmallow caught on his lip, and Trish forced herself to look away. The last thing she should want to think about was kissing Wade Holbrook, the man who let her believe he was married to his pregnant sister.

"Not bad," Wade admitted, though his reserved tone promised some critique to follow. Shadow's nose was now resting on Wade's knee, pleading brown eyes staring up.

"Take another bite," Marti chimed in, reminding Trish they weren't alone. That despite Allen's eagerness to answer the overabundant questions, they still had an audience. "It grows on you."

"So?" Trish asked once he swallowed the last bite.

"It's different. But not horrible."

"Gee, thanks." Trish finished constructing her own, but before she could pick it up with her own fingers, Wade snatched it away and took a bite. "Hey!"

He sent a wicked smile her way, his face carefully tucked away from the rest of the crowd. "Okay, they're a little better than *not bad*." He handed her back the half-eaten s'more. "I'll let you have the rest and make you another. Shadow too, no chocolate please, before she kills me with those pitiful eyes." He rubbed the shepherd along her neck.

There was something intimate about sharing a s'more. Trish found herself staring at the broken edges of the crackers, imagining Wade's lips touching them. "You know what? You can have it." Trish handed off the tray and shoved her roasting fork at Wade. "I think I'm going to turn in for the night." She skittered inside before anyone could talk her into staying, and raced up the stairs.

Once her door was closed behind her, she leaned against it, wondering why she couldn't quite catch her breath.

CHAPTER 5

 **ade**

WADE WAS OFTEN the last one to put out the fire and the first to rise in the morning. Grams slept later these days, which he didn't blame her for. For months after Grandpa was gone, she was rarely out of bed before lunchtime. With Kate hanging around the ranch more often than not, it seemed Grams found a reason to get up early and make a hearty breakfast. But her days of rising before daybreak seemed behind her now.

It was a little after five when Wade snuck out the kitchen door, snatching a lemon poppyseed muffin that Grams had most likely left on the counter for the writers. But they wouldn't miss one;

there were enough stacked there to feed a small army.

Even Shadow gave a yawn at the early hour as she trotted beside Wade. She was eight, and her age showed early in the morning. But between then and her afternoon nap, she was every bit the puppy she'd once been.

"You know, we should be moving that herd. Need to start vaccinations," Allen had said to Wade before he sped off in the ATV. "But instead, Grams has got us as puppets in her photoshoot this afternoon."

"We have to wait another day?" Chet hadn't been given a copy of Grams' itinerary, if his disgruntled expression was any indication.

"Just one more," Wade said.

"Until Grams has us doing the next crazy thing for her writers," Allen tossed in.

"Don't even act like you're put out by this," Wade fired back. Allen was loving every minute of fame, and he knew it.

Near the north pasture, Shadow hopped into the bed of the ATV. Wade took a bite of his muffin before speeding down the road and tossing a bite to his dog.

Chet and Allen would handle feeding and watering the stock. Wade planned to check fences today. It'd been at least a week since anyone had, and it was his turn to make sure there weren't any areas in need of repair. Keeping his cattle safe meant preventing them from escaping, and keeping predators from getting in—one of the first things his grandpa had drilled into the boys.

It was all he'd have time for with his personal-chaperone duties. How Grams even came up with the idea of a personal horseback riding tour of the ranch, this morning of all times, Wade wasn't going to ask. *Such an inconvenience.* Last he saw Trish first thing this morning, she was passed out in the living room recliner. But the guilt trip Grams would give him if he were late was enough to keep him from stalling.

He was still puzzled by Trish's abrupt departure last night. Sure, she seemed a little upset about the misunderstanding, though he thought it was amusing. It might've been better for both of them if she believed he *was* married. But a week was a long time to keep up a silly charade, especially when it included his sister.

After two hours of slow going along the fence line, Shadow was snoring in the back of the ATV, and Wade had yet to spot a single area in need of repair. "Of all the days . . ." One fence post was a little crooked, so he stopped and pulled out a rubber mallet, hoping to right the post without having to pull it out of the ground.

One of the bulls, Ed, raised his head from a hundred yards away. Wade knew it was Ed by the white spot on his chest and goofy tilt of his head. The bull trotted toward him, and Wade instinctively pulled a handful of grass and held out his hand. "Hey there, Ed."

Doing that caused a chuckle as he thought back to when he told his cousin Allen he planned to make a friend of this bull. Allen had laughed at that. "Bet you a hundred bucks this bull will never let you touch him without trying to charge you. In fact, I'd pay a hundred dollars for a ticket to that show!"

It had taken hours of patience, but little by little, Ed warmed up to Wade. It was something about the bull that Wade sensed. He couldn't explain it, but he was good with reading animals, and many trusted him when they wouldn't come within a dozen yards of other hands.

Allen lost the bet at the beginning of the summer.

The bull's soft lips tickled against Wade's palm as the grass disappeared in a few quick chomps. Wade patted Ed's shoulder. "Keeping everyone out of trouble today?" Wade asked.

Allen would get a rise out of Wade talking to Ed. "First you name the bull," Allen had complained. "And now you're petting it? Wade, you know it's a bad idea. We don't usually keep bulls for more than three years."

"Maybe we will this time."

Wade was running operations with his uncle

taking a leave of absence to join his wife on a speaking tour in Europe. Wade suspected his uncle was ready to retire from running the ranch, though he assumed they'd want to live in the main house when they returned. All the more reason to get that cabin renovated quickly. But even from the cabin, Wade could make the important decisions about their animals.

Wade remembered the next thing Allen said, "You're a lot like Grandpa." He was never sure if that was a compliment or a jab, but he shot back, with a cheesy grin, "Grandpa was the best with animals and you know it." Both Grandpa and Ed were special, when Wade thought about it.

Ed *was* special, though it seemed now that Grandpa was gone, only Wade understood that. "You're good at keepin' other animals out and keepin' your buddies in line, aren't ya, Ed?"

Wade wondered what Trish would think of his making friends with a bull. Would she find it charming or ridiculous? He shook that thought away with a wipe of his forehead against his shirt sleeve. It shouldn't matter what she thought. Once this little retreat Grams had cooked up ended, he'd never see Trish Meadows again.

Checking his watch, Wade knew he'd have to turn back soon. Besides, he was out of coffee. "I better get going, Ed, if I wanna keep Grams happy and make that horse-riding tour."

The bull snorted at that.

"I couldn't agree more."

WADE FOUND Trish still passed out in the living room recliner, her laptop open and one hand still on the keyboard. "Good morning, Sunshine!"

Trish squeaked awake, frantically looking around and patting the chair. "Wh-what—"

"Did you sleep out here?"

Trish wiped sleep from her eyes. "I didn't have an extension cord for upstairs."

Taking a closer look, Wade had to wonder how old that monstrosity of a computer was. He was willing to bet the battery worked only minutes, if at all, without being plugged in. "Did you get this for a sweet sixteen present or something?"

Hugging her arms around its edges as if trying to protect it from his insults, she replied, "Maybe it's not a brand-new model, but it works just fine."

Wade sat on the thick arm of the chair and leaned back, amused by the screen. "Quite the enticing story. Is this some new age artist thing? Where you write an entire story with only one letter?"

She quickly closed it on her lap, as though she might have something to hide from him. "What time is it?"

"Seven forty-five."

Trish pushed the recliner's footrest down with her legs. "You've been up for a while, haven't you?"

"Couple hours."

Trish groaned as she tried to escape the chair. From experience, Wade knew it was like trying to escape a pile of soft, man-eating pillows. Add that brick of a computer in her lap, and she struggled. Trish narrowed her eyes. "Don't strain yourself in helping."

"It's much too fun to watch." Wade winked, then strolled off toward the kitchen. The last time their hands had grazed . . . He didn't want to think about it. Best to keep a bubble of space between them just to be safe. "Hurry up and change. You have about ten minutes to get ready and grab a bite to eat."

"Ready for what?"

Over his shoulder he asked, "How close did you read that itinerary Grams made?" When she only yawned, he reminded, "We've got a horseback riding tour of the ranch. Part of your VIP package." He tried to hide his laugh at the groan that ensued.

Wade fixed himself a fresh Thermos of coffee and dug the paper sack marked 'horseback riding lunch' out of the fridge, ignoring the hearts Grams had drawn all over it. If he didn't know better, he'd think Grams was sending them on a date.

"Good, you found the lunch," Kate said with a yawn. "There're drinks in the door, too."

"Grams still asleep?"

60

"She's in the shower. She'll be out soon," Kate reassured. "She put a breakfast casserole together last night for the writers. Has to go in the oven soon."

He wanted to ask his sister if he thought Grams was doing okay with all of this commotion, but Trish was so close, still fighting the recliner. The ranch had been so quiet for so long. It was possible Grams was overwhelmed and hiding. He lost his chance to ask when Trish stepped into the kitchen. He stashed the heart-covered lunch sack behind him, out of Trish's sight line. He didn't want to try explaining that one.

"Hun, you won't want to wear those shoes." Kate rested one hand on her round belly and waved the other toward Trish's feet.

"I don't have any boots with me," Trish admitted. Wade's eyes were immediately drawn to her feet. Some kind of slip-on shoe with jewels thinly covering the narrow straps. "I was hoping to go into town and get a pair, though. Isn't there some tour of the town included in all this?"

"Not until tomorrow. And they're not cheap," Kate warned. "A solid pair of boots will run you a couple hundred dollars." When the color drained from Trish's face, Kate asked, "What size do you wear?"

"Eight."

"Perfect! I have some you can borrow." She sighed. "I haven't been able to get into those since the beginning of my second trimester."

"I don't want to ruin them."

"Nonsense." Kate waved away Trish's concern. "They're work boots. They're meant to get dirty. And hun, you *will* get dirty. You okay with that? If you'd rather stay back here and write—"

"No," Trish said. "I'll go. It's what I signed up for."

"I'm not *that* terrible to be around, am I?" Wade teased, unable to take a steady drink of his coffee because he'd started laughing. "You make it sound like you're coming along to muck out stables."

Trish eyed the spread of muffins on the counter and swiped a blueberry one with icing. "I don't know. You *did* let me think your pregnant sister was your *wife*."

"Wade James Holbrook!" Kate snapped at him, hands on her hips. "Why on earth would you do such a thing?"

"It was a misunderstanding. It's cleared up now. I could never be married to you, even if you weren't my sister." He wrapped her in a hug from behind before she could scold him further in front of the writer, adding, "Ty Riggs is a braver man than I could ever be."

Kate squirmed her way from his hold and turned to Trish. "I'll grab you those boots."

"You *really* didn't bring a pair of boots?" Wade asked. "I mean, even rain boots? They'd be better than those. Does everything you own sparkle?"

He caught the reddening of her cheeks before she ducked her head and focused on peeling the wrapper from her muffin. "It was sort of a last-minute trip."

Wade was surprised at how curious he was at that. "Why did you decide to come?" He had to know. There was something intriguing about this particular writer. Not alluring. But intriguing, he reassured himself. If he was going to be paired up with her all week, he might as well discover her motive.

"Here you go. Brought you some gloves too," Kate interrupted, extending a pair of faded lavender boots toward Trish. "They're pretty worn, but they're perfect for what you'll be doing today."

"Thank you."

"And you'll look cute in them," Kate added with a wink she directed at Wade. He returned it with a scowl. If he didn't know better, both Grams and Kate were cooking up some little scheme, and he wanted none of that. He'd have to make that clear once he and Trish were on their horses away from meddlers.

"Need a cup of coffee before you head out?" Kate asked.

"Yes, please!" Trish's eyes lit up at that prospect.

Kate pointed a finger at him. "Wade, fix the woman a to-go cup." To Trish, she added, "I've got caramel creamer in the fridge. Want some?"

"What you got to fancy up the coffee for, Kate?"

Wade complained. "It's good the way it is. Dark and strong."

"You sure love boring," Trish said with a roll of her eyes that Wade wouldn't admit was in any way cute. What grown woman rolled her eyes? Well, except for his sister. Kate did that every ten minutes, especially now that she was pregnant and what she called *hormonal*.

"On second thought, let me get your coffee." Kate shoved Wade out of the way and stole the Thermos from his hands. "Wyoming in the fall is amazing, but the mornings can be quite chilly. Coffee'll help keep your blood flowing."

"Where you from anyway?" Wade asked, trying to sound casual. But he saw that Kate had perked up at his question. He'd wait to ask any more until they were away from meddling family members.

"Nebraska, most recently." Trish took the cup from Kate, warming her hands on the metal. "Omaha."

City girl. He knew it. That explained all the sparkle. "Know how to ride a horse?" Wade asked, certain he'd not kept the annoyance out of his voice, otherwise Kate wouldn't have glared at him from across the kitchen island.

"Yes." Trish left it at that.

Kate shoved the paper sack at Wade. "Better get going. Grams said the farrier is stopping by after lunch, so you'll need to be back by noon."

Stalling would only subject him to his pushy, irritable sister. It was better to get this over with. If Trish knew how to ride a horse, they could make quick time of the tour. "Let's get to it, then." Wade only hoped she hadn't noticed the pink crayon hearts on the lunch sack.

 *rish*

SHE'D FORGOTTEN the gloves Kate lent her on the kitchen counter, and tried to warm her fingers without Wade noticing her discomfort. They'd only been riding for twenty minutes, but it might as well have been two hours in a blizzard for how cold her fingers felt. Would she even be able to type after this, or would they have to amputate?

"I thought you said you knew how to ride," Wade said as he slowed until they were trotting side by side. "You're sure taking your time, letting Daphne walk you into tree branches."

The sandy brown mare had trotted along easily enough, even if she did tend to meander a bit. But so far, Trish had ducked those occasional branches she steered her into without incident. "I'm wool gathering." She rubbed Daphne along the neck, hoping the mare's mane might help warm her fingers without Wade noticing.

Wade adjusted the brim of his worn Stetson. The color of it reminded her of a faded leather wallet Mindy's grandpa used to carry. Trish had only known him a very short time, but he was always handling that wallet. "Wrong kind of ranch."

"It means I'm taking in the details," Trish said, happy to have something to talk about that made her sound semi-intelligent. It shouldn't matter what this brooding cowboy thought of her, but she didn't want him thinking she was some nitwit. "You know, tucking away ideas for later use." She leaned to her left to avoid a small branch full of yellow leaves. "Some writers call that wool gathering."

"I don't get it."

"Never mind," she said. "It's beautiful out here." Easier to change the subject than brew up another argument. Besides, Wade *was* supposed to be telling her all about the Holbrook Ranch. "Start talking. What's the scoop?"

"The scoop?"

"It's on the itinerary. The one you said I didn't read. You're supposed to tell me all about the history of the family ranch and such."

"You writers are sure an odd sort."

Trish frowned at that. Just what she needed, another Henry. On impulse, she reached into her jacket pocket and pulled out her phone. The bars bounced back and forth between one and three, but it was enough for a text to come through. There was nothing from Henry.

It'd been over two weeks. She should be happy to be rid of someone who didn't support her dreams, but a small part of her wanted him to come around.

"Hey, you even listening?" Wade snapped his fingers.

"Thought my phone dinged."

"Out here?" Wade almost shook his head but seemed to catch himself. "Not likely."

At noticing that small non-gesture, Trish stashed her phone back in her jacket pocket. "I have two bars."

Wade led her to a small clearing a few yards off the trail and stopped the horses. Rolling hills peeked from beneath the cover of trees. A few cattle grazed below. "From here, you can see the entire south pasture," he said, removing his hat. "This was the pasture my great-great-grandfather put his first herd in, same day he bought the ranch. He lived in a tent then, while they built their house."

"A tent?" Trish snuck her phone from her pocket, blushed, but all the same, snapped a couple of pictures. She wanted to have a visual later when she got back to her story. This setting . . . it was perfect. A smile eased across her lips, and for a moment she forgot her fingers were uncooperative icicles.

"Well, the tent was for my great-great-grandmother. She wasn't about to spend all of her nights under the stars, especially with my great-grandpa on the way."

"It's truly a family ranch. I'm impressed."

"Yep. Generation after generation of Holbrooks."

What must it be like, to have a family with such strong roots? She'd never connected with any of her foster families. Mindy was the closest thing she had to family. "I can't imagine what it must be like, living one place your whole life, surrounded by a big family." It sounded wonderful.

It occurred to her that she had yet to meet Wade's parents. Curiosity overcame her instinct to leave the question unasked. "Where are your parents? Did your dad take a turn running the ranch?"

Wade's eyes locked on something invisible in the distance, and he seemed choked for words. "C'mon. More to see."

"Wade—"

"Got to keep moving or I'll miss the farrier."

"Where are we going?" Trish asked, having to yell a bit with Wade ahead of her by a couple of horse lengths.

"To the east pasture. It's where the calves are.

Need to do some checks, make sure everyone's healthy. We were supposed to start the booster inoculations today, but that got delayed." Wade didn't explain further, but Trish suspected she was part of that delay. For as sweet and charming as he acted around his grandma, Wade seemed pretty bitter about the whole chaperone thing. Might this shift be a nerve she struck, asking about his parents?

"Why are you doing this?" she asked.

Wade turned to glance over his shoulder. "Doing what?" But he didn't look directly at her. Better that way. Those blue eyes, the color of a clear Wyoming sky, unsettled her.

She rubbed her hands together again. The sun was rising higher, but they'd stopped in a shaded area. "Pl-playing chaperone?" She tried to fight the chills, but now they were affecting her speech.

"You know, there're gloves in that saddle bag."

"N-now you t-tell me?" Her teeth chattered as they trotted along. She could see cows in the distance, some of them smaller. She could wait until they arrived at the pasture.

"I thought you were tough, being from Nebraska and all."

Trish didn't dignify his jab with a response, nor did she miss that he avoided her question. She settled on a glare to the back of his head, which landed on his black Stetson. She hated to admit how good it looked on him. She allowed herself to study the hat more closely—its shape, its color, how it bobbed up and down with the movement of the horse. How the fleeting rays of sunlight flickered as his horse carried him forward.

She snuck in a picture of that too. All details she could use in her new book. That was all. Anything more, well, there wasn't.

Though she'd lived in several Midwest states, none of them quite resembled this beautiful Wyoming ranch with its rolling hills and their golden hues. Trish brought Daphne to a stop so she could admire the view without falling off and risked snapping a few more pictures. Wade would surely poke fun at her if she landed on the ground. She'd had enough fun with mud for one trip.

"Pretty amazing, huh?"

In her trance, she'd missed him circling his horse back around toward her. Though his eyes were shaded beneath the brim of his Stetson, their deep color caused her to swallow. "Yeah, it's really something. I've been in Omaha for the past few years. Went to college there, never left." Trish frowned at that realization. Why had she chosen a noisy city in which to seek stability? She'd always preferred the quieter life over the bustle. "Kind of forgot what it was like to be somewhere quiet."

"Where did you live, before Omaha?"

Trish was a little taken aback by the question, and the gaze that seemed to hold a flicker of interest in her answer. "Small towns, mostly. Nebraska, Kansas, Iowa." Wherever the system sent her. But she didn't feel like talking about her dull, unhappy childhood. "You've always lived here?"

"Went away to college in Cheyenne." Wade glanced around. "But otherwise, yes."

"On the ranch?" Trish took advantage of her three bars and uploaded a few pictures to social media to reassure Mindy she was making the most of her retreat, including a shot of the back silhouette of the cowboy. Wade would never see it. And maybe as a bonus, Henry would jump to conclusions. He'd yet to unfriend her on social media and was notorious for wasting hours on his.

Wade lifted the reins to lead his horse. "Yep."

"Did your whole family live here? I mean, it's a big house, but that seems like a lot of people under one roof."

"I think I see a limping calf." Wade adjusted his hat. "Wait here. I'll be back."

Trish fought the urge to fire a retort after him for being left behind. Did he think she'd spook the cows or get all squeamish? "Well, Daphne, I guess we have a few minutes to kill." The mare neighed in agreement, then dipped her head to check out the goodies on the ground.

Trish pulled out her phone again, this time to jot down notes about her surroundings—the rolling hills, the way the sun danced along the edges of leaves just starting to turn a golden color, the fresh, crisp air, and a sky so blue she nearly lost herself in staring.

Her eyes dropped on Wade down below her vantage point, hopping off his horse near the gate. Family was a sensitive topic. She'd do well to remember that.

The cattle hardly skittered more than a few steps at Wade's approach. Some didn't move at all. Did all cattle get this used to the people taking care of them, or was there something special about Wade?

When he looked her way and offered a quick wave, Trish ducked her head. To keep herself busy and her eyes off Wade, she tapped around on her phone, deciding to ensure the upload went through. Her post already had six hearts and a couple of comments. Trish lost herself scrolling while she had the bars.

The first response was from Mindy, no surprise: *Who's the cowboy?!? Do you get to keep him?!?*

Before Trish could type out a reply, Wade's voice startled her. "Calf's fine."

Trish nearly fumbled her phone. How had she missed his approach?

"Little guy must've tripped over a rock or some-thing," Wade added. "We have to wean them in a couple of weeks, but we need them healthy. I get a little concerned this time of year." He flashed her that charming smile he'd given the whole group after dinner last night. Whatever had been bothering him earlier seemed fine now. But it was a smile she knew she couldn't trust to be genuine. "Let's grab some lunch. I know a good place to take a break." Wade nodded ahead for Trish to follow and turned his horse.

"Lunch?" Another glance at her phone revealed it was ten-thirteen. "Isn't it a little early for that?"

"By the time we get there, it'll be close enough." He didn't wait to see whether she was going to follow.

They meandered along rough dirt trails, and up and down gently rolling hills with patches of trees for shade. At the top of one hill, Trish had to stop. The landscape spread for miles. Off in the distance, snowcapped mountains appeared in a faded, washed out sort of way. In this beautifully quiet, lost in the most captivating landscape painting she'd ever seen, Trish never wanted to go back to the noisy city again.

"You coming?" Wade called from a few dozen yards ahead.

Easing Daphne downhill on the trail, the river to their left wound through the few scattered trees where Wade was leading them. The sun danced along the tops of the trees, making the whole area appear as if it were on fire.

Wade pulled back on the reins when they reached the shaded riverbank, stopping his horse. "Let's eat. I'm starving!"

"This is beautiful." Trish dismounted, instantly

snapping more pictures with her phone. "Is this river on your land?"

"It's one of the borders," Wade explained. After tying the reins to a nearby fence post, he pulled out a paper sack from his saddle bag, along with a couple bottles of water. "Let's eat."

"It can't possibly be—" But another check of her phone revealed more time had flown by than she realized. It was already eleven. Had she traveled the ranch in a trance, noticing all its beauty but none of the distance?

Wade dropped onto a large fallen tree trunk and set their lunch beside him. A squirrel poked his head around the base of a tree in interest before skittering up it. *Were those hearts drawn on the bag?* "Come, sit down or I'll eat yours, too."

"You wouldn't—"

Mischief twinkled in his eyes, more evident when he removed his hat and the shadows no longer dimmed them from sight. The memory of him handing her the half-eaten s'more last night resurfaced. Trish's heart did an awkward pitter-patter.

She'd barely found a comfortable spot on the log when her phone dinged. "Guess I have two bars out here." It was likely Mindy demanding details about the cowboy in her picture. She meant to set it off to the side and worry about it later.

But the name on the screen nearly made her choke on her sip of water.

Henry: I think this tantrum has gone on long enough. We should talk. Dinner tomorrow?

Her heart pounded at erratic intervals. It'd taken more than two weeks—sixteen days, but she wasn't counting—for Henry to *finally* reach out.

"You really got a signal out here?"

"I told you before, two bars. Sometimes three."

"Must've been a good text. You're grinning like a Cheshire cat."

"It's from Henry." Trish flashed a malicious smirk to the squirrel, nearby now. He'd perked up on that low-hanging branch, studying her instead of Wade with interest and caution. "He doesn't even know I left town. This is going to be great!" The squirrel skittered up a tree at the shift in her tone.

"Who's that?"

Part of her wanted to keep Henry a secret, especially from Wade, though it didn't make sense. Telling him—maybe adding in a few embellishments —would make it clear she wasn't interested. "Boyfriend of sorts. Well, we've been dating for six months. But I broke things off a couple of weeks ago."

Wade continued to eat his sandwich. He didn't ask for details, but he didn't stop her either, so Trish kept on.

"Henry doesn't consider writing to be a realistic

career option. Says writing books is a waste of time. He thinks I need to work in an office all my life. Build a *real* career." She left out the part about his skipping out on her celebration.

"Sounds horrible," Wade said. "Who wants to work in an office their whole life?"

"Exactly!" They shared an innocent smile. At least Trish thought it was innocent until her pulse betrayed her. "What's for lunch?" She dug in the bag that was most definitely covered in pink crayon hearts.

"Roast beef sandwiches."

Trish fished one out, discovering a container of apple slices too. "Once I get a chance to talk to that literary agent about my book, that'll show Henry he was wrong. If she happens to like my story, I might get an offer to work with her. You know, a contract and all that. Contracts is a language Henry understands."

"What do you see in this guy Hank anyway?"

"Henry." Trish locked eyes with Daphne, who was definitely eyeing her apple slices. Setting down her sandwich, Trish carried a handful over to the horse. "He's practical, has a successful career, is great with numbers, very organized, stable . . ."

Wade flashed an amused smile her way. "You sound like you're reading his resume."

"He's a good guy," Trish defended, though the words left a sour taste in her mouth.

"Don't sound so sure."

Trish giggled at the tickle of Daphne's lips on her hands. *What would it be like to have my own horse someday?* She gave Daphne some love, kissed her on the muzzle, then turned back to her lunch with the frown gone. "I miss being around horses," she said, eager to change the subject.

"Did you have horses, before you moved to Omaha?"

"No." Trish took a bite of her sandwich. "In one of the towns I lived in when I was thirteen, I worked at a stable for a whole summer. It's where I learned to ride."

"You moved around a lot." Not a question.

"Yep." Trish took a few more photos of the river with the fall colors in the frame. She'd have a few hours to write before the photoshoot. With all the pictures and notes she'd taken, she couldn't wait to get to her laptop. "Never even had a dog. Speaking of, where's Shadow?"

"Allen needed her help with some steers this morning."

"She's a working dog?"

"When she wants to be." Wade hopped to his feet. Trish too rose and got to work till everything was cleaned up. "Spoiled is what she really is." They shared another smile, and Trish swore her heart tried to leap up into her throat. What was wrong with her? There could be nothing here. Wade was only assigned to entertain her, most likely against his will. By next week, she'd never see him again.

"Do we need to head back?" Trish asked, folding the heart-covered lunch bag into smaller and smaller squares.

"Farrier's due soon. I need to help Chet and Allen for a few hours too, or I'll never hear the end of it." Wade waited until she had mounted Daphne before he asked, "You text that Howard fellow back?"

Trish leveled him with a playful glare. "Henry." Gloves no longer needed, she shoved them into her pocket. "And no. He can wait." The least she could do after he made her wait over two weeks.

"Good. Let's get back, then."

Trish couldn't decide if hearing from Henry made her excited or irritated. She'd dreamt about him reaching out for the past two weeks, full of apologies and remorse at ever doubting her dream. Why didn't it feel as good as she'd imagined it would?

 *ade*

WADE FELT he'd been saved when the farrier's truck pulled into the ranch just as he and Trish made it back. He needed some space from the alluring writer who was starting to mess with his head. He shouldn't care one way or the other, but he didn't like this Henry guy one bit.

"How was your date?" Allen nudged him hard in the shoulder once Trish disappeared back toward the house.

"Not a date." Wade led Daphne back to her stall, relieved Trish put up little resistance once he encouraged her to scoot off and get some writing in, saying it was fine that she let him take care of her horse. Daphne had been a bit dejected to leave her new friend. Odd how quickly they bonded. She was usually indifferent to most folks.

"Oh, come on. Your sack lunch had *hearts* on it for crying out loud." Allen laughed loud and boisterously. Had Allen seen the handoff just before Trish turned to make her way into the house? Then it dawned on him.

"You drew those." Wade shook his head and shoved his way around his cousin to hang up the saddle. "Should've known." He felt the slightest edge of relief that Grams wasn't trying to set him up. He didn't need her, or anyone for that matter, meddling in his love life. He was happy the way things were.

"You can't tell me you hated spending time with that cute romance author." Following Wade back to the stall, Allen leaned against the wooden door. "You'd be crazy not to be interested in her."

"Then I'm crazy." Wade ran gentle but firm strokes with the horse brush over an approving Daphne. He didn't get Allen's pushiness. Trish would be gone in a week. And it was no secret between him and his cousins that he wasn't interested in dating anyone seriously. "Why does it matter to you so much? She'll be gone for good in a few days."

"Then you better hurry up before you miss your chance."

"Not interested."

"You could always ask her to stay."

Wade almost dropped the brush, catching it in a tumble. "Knock it off, Allen. She's pining after some guy back home." Daphne nudged him with her soft muzzle to continue the gentle strokes that had stopped.

"Heard all about that from one of the other writers. *They* say she dumped him. Those ladies are on a mission to make sure she leaves him dumped."

"Where's that brother of yours?" Wade asked, scanning the stable for Chet. He was irritated enough that he didn't have time to work on his cabin tonight. He didn't need all this from Allen, too.

"Went to meet George, since you were too busy putting away your girlfriend's horse."

Wade considered throwing the horse brush but didn't feel like retrieving it. He found an apple core on the ground and threw it at Allen instead. "Stop talking like that, okay? You'll give her ideas, Allen." In truth, Wade was more worried about another misunderstanding. She'd been kind enough to forgive him for the one about Kate, but she might not forgive another. Especially one that had the chance of embarrassing her.

"Fine, I'll quit." Allen threw his hands up in surrender. "But if you're not interested in her, you won't mind if I give it a shot. Might serenade her with a good ol' country song."

A strange, painful tinge coursed through Wade. He shook it off. "You're not her type."

Allen laughed again. "You've spent a few hours with her, and suddenly you know her type?" He threw the core back, hitting Wade in the shoulder hard enough to leave a mark.

"Ow!"

"We'll see about her type." Allen backed away. "Gotta go get cleaned up for our photoshoot with those lady writers," he added with a wink.

Wade groaned, catching Daphne's attention. Why couldn't Allen leave all things to do with Trish alone? His cousin had always enjoyed riling him up a bit, and usually it had to do with some sort of competition. But it'd been college since they competed for a girl, and Wade wasn't about to play that game now. The first prickles of irritation poked at him.

Wade patted Daphne, then slipped out of the stall to find the farrier. He was supposed to be running things around here with his uncle out of the country. He couldn't shirk all his responsibilities, even if it meant dealing with a crotchety farrier. George was great with horses, but not so much with people.

"Let's get this over with," he mumbled, secretly hoping the farrier would keep him too busy to join in for the photoshoot. Except the image of Allen snuggled up close to Trish for a picture, in his most expensive cologne, made Wade see a little bit of red.

~

WADE'D JUST STEPPED out of the shower when he heard the house phone ringing. Grams wasn't a fan of cell phones, and though she had one Kate bought her last Christmas, she rarely turned it on. That forced most people to call the landline.

"Grams?" he called out into the empty kitchen. The farrier hadn't been in a hurry earlier, making Wade a little bit late. The Holbrook Ranch had been the last on his list for the day, but Wade didn't want to leave him alone in the stable. Mostly, he didn't want George to still be around for this. All they needed was him to come looking for one of them. What would he think, finding them all in the backyard taking romance novel cover-worthy pictures? It would be too much to explain to crotchety ol' George.

On the fourth ring, Wade zipped around the kitchen island and picked up the phone from the wall receiver. Grams had been having problems with her answering machine lately, so this might be her best chance for a message.

"Wade, how you been?"

"Uncle Bill. Where you callin' from today?" Wade leaned against the counter and crossed his legs.

"Barcelona."

Wade glanced at the clock on the stove. "It's kinda late there, isn't it? Where's Aunt Tabby?"

"She's got a couple days off before the next events, so she's at a bar down the street from our hotel with some fans." Bill rambled on a bit more about the speaking event and the mass of fans. Wade's aunt was a motivational speaker in high demand. She'd been doing a circuit in Europe for the past several weeks and her popularity was exploding.

"Sounds like you two are having a great time."

"We get to take it easy between events. Since it's all paid for, can't ask for more than that. How's things? Heard Grams talked you into playing an escort to some writer gal." Bill cackled until he coughed. Too many years of smoking behind him.

"Chaperone," Wade corrected. "We're actually due out back for a photoshoot, of all things. Guess Grams wants them to have something to remember us by. Can't imagine why anyone would want photographic evidence of knowing Allen," Wade joked. "He's lapping up his temporary fame."

"Of course he is." Wade couldn't discern whether there was disapproval in Bill's tone. "Look, I need you to tell Grams to get hold of me. She can send an email so I know when it's a good time to call back. I ran into someone today interested in buying some land out there."

It should have struck Wade as odd that his uncle had coincidentally found someone wanting to buy land in Wyoming while he was halfway around the world. Wade's stomach twisted uneasily. "You think she knows some folks selling land around here?"

"I described that north pasture to this guy I met today, and you should have seen his eyes light up. Look, he's willing to pay cash. More'n it's worth, too. It's just a hundred acres. Small parcel of land. And it would set Grams up for years if she sold it at that price."

Wade thought he might get dizzy from this conversation. His grandpa had to be turning in his grave with the thought of a single acre being sold. "Why the north pasture?" Bill, like Grams, didn't know how much work Wade had been putting into that cabin. Bill must have remembered how Wade mentioned his interest in someday claiming that parcel as his own; mentioned it more than once.

"It's got the best view." Chatter in the background and the closing of a door announced his aunt's return.

"It also has some of the best grazing land we have."

"All our pastures are good for that."

The conversation reminded him of the many arguments his uncle and grandpa had about how to run the ranch. Grandpa cared about the animals, found the highest form of pride and reward in a hard day's work, loved the land. Bill, on the other hand, liked to find excuses to skate out of work early.

Always interested in something that might bring in *big money*.

"Look, if someone took down that old cabin, there's a decent plot of land to build a new house perfect for a bachelor. Just tell Grams to check her email so I can figure out a good time to call her back."

Wade had no such intention, but it was the easiest way to get Uncle Bill off the phone. With any luck, that buyer would find land somewhere else to spend his money, before the possibility was ever mentioned to Grams. "I'll tell her. Check her email."

"Wade, you know this is good for her. Money's tight. Selling that parcel would take that burden off her shoulders for years."

Grams always did the books. Wade gave her information about costs and expenses. Had brief conversations with her about a good time to buy and sell. But she'd never let him *see* the books. Maybe what Bill was saying had some truth in it. "Enjoy Barcelona, Uncle Bill."

Wade hung up and stared at the wall mount receiver, muttering curses on his way back to the bathroom. He'd planned to shave his two-day stubble, but now he felt too irritated to wield something as dangerous as a razor blade. Grams would forgive him the light beard. She wouldn't be happy if he came out there with bloody nicks all over his cheeks.

Wade anchored himself with two hands on the edges of the sink and bowed his head to catch his breath. Nausea slammed him at the thought of Grams not having enough money. Was Grams really holding this writers' retreat in some attempt to increase revenue and not just a dream fulfilled as she made it out to be? Things had been tight this season, but tight enough that she would even consider selling a single acre? He didn't want to believe it.

rish

"Gather 'round now," Lina shouted at the gaggle of cowboys and writers milling near the picturesque gazebo she and Kate had draped with beautiful orange flowers. Later, Trish would have to ask what that flower was called. She could use that type of detail in her story. "We're just about ready. Want to get these in before it gets dark."

"Isn't this exciting?" Glenda wore a smile brighter than the sun. "I've never had my picture taken with a cowboy before. Can't wait to send it to my husband!" She rubbed her hands together, as if this might be the greatest little scheme ever.

Trish searched for Wade but didn't see him anywhere. She frowned.

"Don't worry." Kate patted Trish's shoulder from behind, pausing briefly on her way to the gazebo. "Wade's on his way. He smelled worse than the barn on a hot day. I sent him in to shower."

Trish smiled back. "I wasn't worried." But she was. Because a picture with Wade was just the ticket to get Henry's blood boiling. Especially after she ignored his last text. A call earlier with Mindy confirmed her plan was the right one.

"Henry'll go ballistic if you post a picture with that yummy cowboy! With his arm around you *after* you ignored his text?" Mindy had been practically bursting with evil laughter. Henry didn't post much online about himself. His profile was squeaky clean and professional. But he stalked Facebook every spare second. No way he'd miss a post like that. "But Trish, why do you care what Henry thinks?"

"I don't." She'd almost meant it.

"Absolutely. I believe that. Now go get dolled up. I packed some of that Romantic Allure perfume of mine you always try to steal. *Use it.*"

In the writers' huddle, Trish heard Marti tell Glenda, "I'm still trying to decide which platform to focus on." That brought Trish back to the present. "It's a tie between Twitter and Facebook. I don't think I can keep up with both. One of them has to go."

"Platform?" Trish repeated, the word new to her in any sort of writerly context.

"Of course! Agents find writers more appealing if they have an established social media platform." Marti wore a big smile, as if she'd just shared a best kept secret. "You know, a following."

"But I haven't published anything," Trish stammered. "Who'd follow me?" *Besides Mindy.* Well, at least she'd have one fan. Panic bubbled in Trish's chest, the air suddenly hard to breathe. Was the literary agent expecting her to have a platform? What if someone already tried looking her up and couldn't find her?

"You don't *need* to publish to start building a platform," Glenda chimed in. "In fact, don't wait." She leaned down, digging through her denim satchel. "You shouldn't anyway. Here." She lifted a paperback to Trish. "Have a read. It talks about the platform-building thing. Social media was a foreign concept when I first started publishing. But if *I* can figure it out, I know you can."

"Oh, that's a good one," Marti said as she got a good look at the paperback. "I've read that one a couple of times. Good chapter in there about newsletters, too. Get that going right away!"

"Th-thank you," said Trish, overwhelmed by a whole new set of tasks she never knew existed for an author.

"Of course, dear. We writers have to stick

together, you know." Glenda flashed a smile at Trish, then asked, "How's your new story coming? Any words in today? We missed you at our morning session, but Lina said you had a horseback date. Riding with a certain cowboy."

"I wouldn't call it a date."

"Why not?" Glenda jumped in, adding a wink. "You're both single."

The sun was sure hot this late afternoon. Trish fanned herself with the social media book. "I'm not ready to start dating again." It was the easiest answer she could give. "Henry—"

"—is a dud," Marti interrupted.

"I finished chapter three of my new book," Trish said, hoping to divert the conversation away from the men in her life. "Decided my poor heroine needed to land herself in a good mud puddle, right in front of the handsome cowboy."

"Inspired by true events?" Glenda nudged her shoulder.

"You could say that."

While Lina directed Allen and Chet to hang some last-minute decorations around the gazebo, Trish asked Glenda, "How does it feel to have twelve published books? That has to be such an amazing feeling!"

"It's an addiction, really. Like potato chips. You can't have just one."

"She's right," Marti agreed. But most of her

attention was on the gazebo. She rocked on both feet, her eyes trailing constantly between Allen and Chet. Mostly Allen. In all reality, Marti was probably old enough to be Allen's mother, but Trish wasn't going to spoil her fun little crush by saying so.

"I hope I'll be like both of you one day." Trish repeated, "Several books published." So much was riding on her meeting with the literary agent. And here she didn't even have a platform! Tonight, as she'd been coached, she'd do her homework on the agent. *And* start her platform. *Maybe Mindy could help?* She couldn't wait to dazzle the agent with her novel. It would be such a wonderful post to add to her wall, along with her cozy cowboy pic.

"The publishing world is changing, honey," Glenda said. "The sky's the limit. Write a good book. Then write another. Keep that plan on repeat and you're set."

"Aren't you nervous for your meeting?" Trish asked, hoping she wasn't the only one. But how could someone like Glenda with a dozen published titles to her name be afraid of an agent? One she clearly didn't seem to need to be successful. Trish had stalked Glenda last night and found a couple of best-seller ribbons online. Or Marti? A quick search revealed six of her published titles with hundreds of positive reviews.

"Sure. It's always a little nerve-racking talking to

someone with that kind of power. But at the end of the day, she's just another person like you and me."

At Lina's clapping, Glenda and Trish turned their heads together. Marti practically sprinted onto the stage. "Guess she's first in line," Glenda said with a hearty laugh.

Trish couldn't help it. She searched again for Wade. No sign of him.

"You hoping to make that Henry guy jealous?" Glenda asked.

"You can get his name right," Trish mumbled with a chuckle. When she met Glenda's confused gaze, she added a, "Never mind." Trish adjusted the neckline of her floral blouse. It was simple yet elegant, a piece Mindy helped her pick out for a special dinner with Henry.

"You look distant." Glenda asked, "What're you thinking about, dear?"

"This shirt." Trish pulled a pinch of fabric away from her shoulder. "I bought it thinking I'd be wearing it to dinner when Henry proposed."

Glenda glanced quite obviously at Trish's ring-less finger. "What were you celebrating instead?"

"His latest promotion. He gets a couple each year."

"It's a beautiful blouse. I think you'll get some *proper* use of it." Glenda winked before Lina ushered her away to the gazebo.

"Forget about this guy for an evening," Kate said

from behind Trish, startling her. "He doesn't deserve the time you're spending thinking about him. And you deserve better than to settle."

Folding her arms, Trish scanned the backyard again. Shadow came bounding out the back door. Her tail wagged at the sight of Trish, but a squirrel diverted her attention before she could make it over for one of Trish's ear rubs. Shadow chased it up a tree and danced around the trunk with bright, victorious eyes.

"Shadow, leave that poor squirrel alone!" Kate called as she moved toward a chair. Shadow wagged her tail with more vigor at the attention.

It made Trish mourn never having a dog. Maybe it was time to change that. It might mean going home for lunch every day until her writing could support her full time, but she was fine with that arrangement. Only Henry seemed to think one needed to work ten-hour days without breaks to make any day count.

"You look great, by the way." Kate sat with undisguised relief, waving a hand at Trish's outfit. Her long, flowing skirt whooshed like a parachute as she dropped. "I can take a few shots with your phone if you want. Help you make that jerk back at home wish he'd supported your dreams."

Does everyone know about Henry? Trish couldn't decide if she felt violated or touched. Rather than ask, she changed the subject. "How did your grandma talk the guys into this? Can't tell me they volunteered. That one over there looks like someone stole his birthday."

"Oh, Chet? He always looks grumpy, even when he's happy." Kate adjusted her skirt around her ankles, finally resting her hands on her belly. "Now Allen, you better believe he's eating this up. You writers make him feel like he's a celebrity. He's a real charmer, that one. I'd be surprised if he hasn't hit on you yet. Let me apologize in advance for when that happens."

"This was all your grandma's idea?" Trish waved her hand in a circle, unable to keep her eyes from falling to the back door of the house in the process. Someone had let Shadow out, but he had yet to appear.

"Grams loves romance novels. Always has. After Grandpa passed, she boxed up every single paperback she owned and donated them to the library. I'm talking dozens of boxes. We thought she'd never come out of it. But she dreamed up this retreat a couple of months ago, and here we are." Kate craned her neck around Trish, looking at something near the gazebo. "Looks like she needs my help. Should've known better than to sit down."

Trish asked, "Need a hand?"

Kate gave a good effort to stand, but the seat's legs seemed to sink into the soft earth, and angled down. She finally accepted Trish's extended hand, and together they got her back on her feet. "Thanks.

This child needs to get here already, if only so I can get out of a chair by myself again."

"How's your story coming?" Lizzie asked as she joined Trish. She was adjusting her curled hair in a handheld mirror, but the wind was doing a better job at whipping it around, no matter what she did. Lizzie still looked like a romance cover model, either way. Especially in that cute sundress, and Trish told her so. "Get anything written this afternoon?"

"Another chapter." Trish loved this so much. The ability to talk to other writers who understood how exciting it was to write new words. Mindy, so supportive, had tried her best to be enthusiastic. But she didn't quite understand the excitement of finishing a new chapter or having a plot break-through. "How about you?"

"My cowboy is creating all kinds of havoc." Lizzie winked at Trish. "I'm loving every word!"

The back door slammed, and Trish's attention shifted to Wade headed their way. He looked much like the picture Lina had chosen for the website advertisement. Utterly delicious, and perfect for making an ex jealous enough to stew. Well, except for the scowl.

"Yum!" Lizzie danced her fingers along the railing. "Can't wait to get my picture with *that* one. He's my favorite." She touched Trish's arm, then hurried off toward the gazebo with Lina waving her over.

"Is it over yet?" Wade asked when he stepped into the shade next to Trish.

"Hardly." It was the only word she could choke out. Had he put on cologne too? "You're the main attraction."

"Is that so?"

"All the writers say so." It was true. They'd all been drooling at the thought of getting a fun, intimate picture with *the* Wade Holbrook. And judging by the way Lina was staging the couples in the gazebo, there would be some intimate shots. The thought of Wade's arm draped around her sent shivers up Trish's arms.

"Wade," Lina hollered. "Over here! Trish, you too."

Trish took a deep breath. Why was she nervous? It had to be because of Henry seeing any photo she posted. Her desire to make him a little jealous. But her eyes trailed after Wade looking too good in that fitted blue shirt that complemented his eyes so well. His long days on the ranch no doubt accounted for that muscle definition.

"Okay, let's have you two lean against the post," Lina directed. Kate rested against the gazebo railing in the opposite corner, camera strapped around her neck while she waited for Lina to position her subjects.

Wade let his hip drop against the post, folding his arms in a manner tinged with sullenness. His scowl had yet to improve, but it made him attractive. *Better than his fake smile anyway.* Trish wondered if they'd use that picture right there to attract the next slew of attendees. Every romance writer loved a sullen cowboy. They'd have retreats booked for the rest of the year.

"Trish," Lina directed, pulling her by the elbow toward Wade. "Let's have you stand next to him. Kind of tuck you in there." Lina used both hands to guide Trish right where she wanted her, which was apparently with her back flush against that rock-solid chest. "Wade, drop your hands. One behind her back." Lina guided his other hand, placing it on her shoulder.

Could he feel how wobbly she was on her feet or how her breathing was becoming erratic? Surely everything was trembling. It was all a ruse, Trish had to remind herself. Everyone cared so much about Lina. This was for her.

"Dip your head a bit," Lina said to Wade. Trish felt the brim of his hat brush the top of her head, his breath tickling her neck. She shivered. Lina gave out a few more commands, tweaked some limb placements, and finally backed up. But Trish couldn't understand the words that left her mouth. Not with that breath on the back of her neck making her dizzy. Displaced.

Lina clapped her hands together. "Now, you two. Smile at the camera."

Kate snapped continuously, even when Trish took a moment to close her eyes. It was a failed attempt to catch her breath.

"Perfect!" Lina called over her shoulder, "Glenda, your turn! Wade, you stay put."

Trish broke free from Wade's hold, her legs as reliable as overcooked noodles. She held on to the railing until she reached the opening.

"Hey." Kate handed Trish's cell phone to her. "Got a few good ones."

"Th-thanks." Trish's eye caught a trail through the trees as Glenda posed with Wade for another photo. She needed to get away from everyone—and from the cowboy who was scrambling her ability to form words.

Looking over her shoulder to ensure no one was paying attention or trying to follow, Trish slipped into the cover of the yellowing foliage and followed the narrow dirt path until the laughing voices behind faded.

Finding a quiet place by a stream Trish suspected connected to the main river, she dropped to a seated position on a bed of soft leaves. What was happening? Being that close to Wade had her feeling as if she were plugged into a transformer. She'd never felt that kind of electricity with Henry.

Trish pulled her phone out, her trembling fingers flipping through the pictures Kate had snuck in for her. Those blue eyes staring at the camera made her come unglued. Mindy—and all of social media for that matter—would eat this up. But Trish was having trouble formulating a post.

"You get lost?" A voice startled her, and her phone tumbled to the ground.

Brushing the dirt from the screen, Trish wasn't surprised to see Wade standing at the trail ending, but she'd really hoped to be alone. Had Lina sent him, or had he darted for an escape route the first chance he got? "Nope." Trish pointed behind him. "The way back is through that trail."

"Grams was worried."

The way he wouldn't quite meet her eyes left Trish suspicious. "Was she now?"

"Allen offered to come to your rescue, but one of your author buddies practically lassoed him before he could get away." Wade leaned against a tree. He was missing his Stetson. Trish wondered who had it in their possession.

"That'll be Marti. I think she has the hots for your cousin."

Ignoring her comment, Wade nodded at the phone in her hands. "Get any reception out here?" he asked.

"Some." She folded her hands around her cell.

"You must have some sort of super powered cell phone," he teased. "Missing your city comforts?"

"Nope." Trish might feel differently in a couple of days, but so far she loved the disconnection. She hadn't once wondered how the office was functioning without her there to put out all the fires. "I like the quiet."

"Even though we're hours from the nearest mall?"

Trish leveled him with a glare, pushing up off the ground. "I've just about had enough with you and your assumptions of who you think I'm supposed to be." She stormed past him, careful to avoid physical contact. That would only make her head spin. She didn't need the extra layer of confusion.

"I didn't mean—"

Trish tossed a hand up in the air, failing to turn around and give him the benefit of eye contact. Maybe she was overacting to his teasing, but one thing was certain. Being too close to Wade was dangerous.

 *ade*

WADE FOUND Grams in the kitchen an hour after the photoshoot activities were finished. She was stuffing a blanket into a backpack. "Grams, you running away from home?" But his chuckle was pitiful at best. He couldn't stop Uncle Bill's conversation from replaying in his mind.

"You have a moonlit walk tonight. I forgot to remind you. With Trish."

"A what?" He'd looked at the itinerary this morning, just to be sure he knew what his day entailed. "After the photoshoot, I'm supposed to be a free man." Because it'd been too dark to work on his cabin, he planned on lighting a fire on the patio and sitting. Alone. In the quiet. "There's no moonlit walk on the schedule."

"You must not have a copy of the revised schedule." Grams stuffed a flashlight in the bag, then scanned the kitchen counters, looking for what, Wade couldn't guess. "I added it a couple of days ago. Did I forget to give it to you?"

"Grams, I'm beat." Wade's arms still tingled when he recalled Trish shoved up close to him for the photoshoot. He really needed some space tonight. "Doesn't she have writing or something she needs to get done?"

"Oh, Wade." Lina paused her packing and brought out the pitiful blue eyes. It was a look Wade knew better than to test. She could turn into a puddle of tears. "It's just that Trish was so excited when I reminded her. Your grandpa and I used to take moonlit walks on the ranch all the time. I thought it would be great writing inspiration. Might be a highlight for future retreats . . ."

Future retreats? Thinking of Bill's message, Wade wrapped her in a hug and kissed her forehead. "Okay, Grams. I'll go grab her." Anything to keep her from falling apart. It'd been a couple of months since he last witnessed those grief-stricken tears. He couldn't bear them tonight, especially if he was the cause.

"Thank you, Wade." Grams squeezed him back,

then pushed him toward the doorway. "She's in the living room."

Trish was back in the man-eating recliner, footrest up, fingers furiously typing. Earbuds must have blocked him out. Wade wondered why she was downstairs writing again instead of in her room. There was an outlet beneath the writing desk. But, he supposed, that wooden chair *was* a little stiff.

He sidled toward her, waiting for her to look up and spot him. He wondered what it would take to get out of this moonlit walk without upsetting Grams. "Hey." He gently kicked the bottom of the chair to get her attention. Trish startled, her brick of a laptop wobbling on unsteady knees.

"Don't do that!" Trish pulled out her earbuds once her laptop was steady. "Is that a hobby or something, sneaking up on me? Being some cowboy ninja?"

"Cowboy ninja?" Wade laughed. It was too ridiculous not to. "You ready to go on our walk?"

Trish looked longingly at her screen, then at Wade.

"It would mean a lot to Grams," he added in a low voice. Was he really trying to convince her to go? Wouldn't Grams forgive him if the writer was the one opting out?

"Is it nine already?"

"'Fraid so."

"I'll meet you out back?"

Wade nodded, then headed for the kitchen to see how much more Grams had packed for this little adventure. He wondered if there really was a revised itinerary, but he reminded himself Allen had been the prankster who drew hearts on the sack lunch, not Grams. Seemed most likely that Grams was missing Grandpa and this was her way of honoring his memory.

"I packed a blanket and a few extra things," Grams said. "Probably best to take her down that trail by the barn. It'll be lit up the best. And there's that fire pit at the clearing if you decide to stay out a bit. Keep you two warm."

The click of claws on the tile alerted them to Shadow's presence. She stopped halfway into the kitchen and stretched with a loud groan. She'd been napping under the dining room table. Wade considered leaving her at the house as she normally made her way onto the end of his bed by nine-thirty and passed out cold. But her brown eyes widened in interest at the pack on the counter.

"You want to join us for a walk, girl?" Wade asked. Having his dog along might help to make the walk less . . . awkward. That romance angle had to be what Grams was going for. If he brought Shadow, she could wedge herself between them. Prevent another misunderstanding Wade couldn't apologize his way out of.

Shadow wagged her tail, it thudding against the cupboards.

"Of course she's excited," Trish said as she entered the kitchen and rubbed Shadow along her neck and behind her ears. "She wasn't stuck on the ranch all day with *you*." There was a twinkle in her eyes at those possibly flirtatious words.

Lina laughed from behind him, and Wade caught the red flush of Trish's cheeks. "I know being saddled with my grandson for an entire day can be a little much." She chuckled. "But you two have a go at it. Make it special. Should be quite inspiring for some evening writing, Trish. Trust me, I know. It's a magical walk."

"I'm sure it's gorgeous in the light of the moon."

"It absolutely is. I was telling Wade just a bit ago how my late husband and I used to take walks all the time when we were younger." Wade turned at those words to make sure Grams wasn't about to cry. He couldn't bear it tonight, not with his own emotions charged.

"Sounds like a great scene to write."

"Every activity for this retreat is designed to inspire romantic scenes for your books. I couldn't wrangle up my other two grandsons tonight, so this moonlit walk is a VIP package special. Wade has graciously accepted to be your tour guide. He'll keep you safe." Lina patted the bag on the counter and

shoved it toward Wade. "You two should be all set."
She slipped out of the room with a glowing smile.

"Safe?" Trish repeated.

"From coyotes," Wade answered. "Bears."

"There are no bears around here," Trish
interjected.

Wade shrugged. "Okay. If you say so. If you're
too afraid to go—" he started, but Trish cut him off.

"Never said that. Plus, we have Shadow." She
knelt down and hugged his dog. Odd. Shadow didn't
normally appreciate that kind of affection, but with
Trish she was eating it up. Shadow licked Trish on
the cheek, and she giggled. "When do we leave?"

∾

TRISH

THIS WAS A BAD IDEA. Like *very* bad. One of those
ideas that got a girl into trouble. Trish really
needed to track down that itinerary so she had
more time to prepare for any more unexpected
events Lina had planned. She'd been happily
typing away on her new Chapter Four when Lina
tapped her on the shoulder and mentioned something about a revised itinerary and this moonlit
walk.

The concept *was* romantic. It *would* make a

great scene to write. But walking under a moonlit sky with Wade? Alone?

Trish's overactive imagination ran away with her. It always did. The starry sky. The singing of crickets. A gentle breeze. This strong man who filled out his T-shirt so well. Even if it was covered with a jacket to ward off the cold. A jacket the hero in her story would surely give to her heroine if she caught a chill.

This overactive imagination was the very reason Mindy had insisted Trish would make a good romance novelist.

"You keep moving that slow and you'll get left behind." Wade stopped a few dozen feet ahead of her on the dirt-packed trail and waited for her to catch up. Shadow zipped circles around them, weaving in and out of the trees.

"Such a gentleman." Trish had been a little distracted by it all. A girl could fall in love out here—her heroine could fall in love out here—on a moonlit walk. Lina was right.

"Grams gave us the long trail. The slower you go, the longer we'll be out."

"Rearrange those words a little, and you might make a semi-decent romance novel hero."

Wade shook his head. "I have some work to do early in the morning."

Trish thought it might be a bad time to remind him they were supposed to have breakfast in town tomorrow. She'd let his grandma spoil his good mood.

Deciding she was close enough, apparently, Wade turned and kept walking. So far, there'd been glimpses of him that made him seem warm and friendly. But they seemed rare amid this grumpier, put-out version.

"Why did you agree to this?" Trish asked, remembering how he dodged her question earlier today. "You run the ranch. Surely the other cowboys could entertain the writers. How did you get roped into being a personal escort?"

"That a little pun there?"

"You're smiling, aren't you?" Trish could only guess with the way he faced forward. But when he turned his head, the white of his teeth showed in the moonlight, curving into a not-so-reluctant smile. Trish nearly collided into him, unaware his feet had stopped moving. She wasn't ready to be so close to him again, not after that photoshoot. Her mind was bouncing around like a fly trapped inside on a hot summer night.

"The path gets a little tricky for a bit." Wade adjusted the straps of the backpack. He seemed to hesitate before he reached out his hand, offering, "I know the trail pretty well."

"Is this on *the itinerary?*" Trish meant it in a teasing way, but with the way his lips straightened into a grimace, she regretted her words. She took his hand before he could withdraw it. Ahead of where he stood, she could see the path descend. With how dark it was ahead, she had no idea how far down it went or what might be lurking below. Electric tingles raced through their joined hands and up her arm, and for a moment, she forgot how to use coherent words.

"You good?" came through the dimness.

Trish just nodded. But she so wasn't. Between her overactive romance writer imagination, the memory of being wrapped in his arms earlier, and now a moonlit walk, she was in so much trouble when it came to this cowboy.

CHAPTER 10

 **ade**

THIS WAS A BAD IDEA, and Wade knew it. He never should have agreed to this chaperone thing. Maybe Grams would've been disappointed, but could he have offered to make it up in other ways? Group participation, for instance. Instead, he was alone in the moonlight with a beautiful woman under the cover of trees.

"Romance novels, huh?" he asked, desperate to distract himself from the sensation of Trish's touch. It was safest to keep their hands connected. He knew this trail with his eyes closed, but someone unfamiliar might have a hard time navigating it in the daylight with its unruly tree roots and random steep drop-offs. Grams would kill him if he brought her back damaged. Add an energetic German shepherd running zigzags around them, and anyone stumbling onto this path at night was bound to break a bone or at least twist an ankle.

"I think I should've signed a waiver," Trish mumbled. "Yes, romance novels. I'm sure you read them by the boat load."

Wade chuckled at that poor attempt at a joke. Her grip tightened each time she had to step over a tree root or navigate a sharp turn. Trish was much too close to him. His heart threatened to break through his chest.

If Grams offered this tour again, Wade would be smarter. He'd certainly rule out this trail. He could imagine one of the other writers fawning all over him and purposely falling against him, trying out that whole damsel-in-distress thing. At least Trish was trying to take it all on her own, only accepting help when necessary. He admired her independence.

"Can't say I've ever picked one up."

"Do you read?" Trish asked, her breath seemed heavier from the difficult path. "Books, that is?"

"Not much." Working long hours on both the ranch and his cabin, well, it didn't leave much leisure time. When he did have it, he preferred to sit in silence. Revel in it.

"You're missing out."

"How's that?" This talking was good. A distraction from the heat of her touch.

"They're an escape from reality."

"I like my reality."

Trish stopped, yanking him back a step as she did. He muttered under his breath when he nearly slipped on a stray branch. "You've never wanted *anything* different? Or even wondered?"

They should keep walking, but she looked so beautiful in the moon's glow. He couldn't deny that, no matter how much he wanted to. It seemed to paralyze him; it took a moment to answer. "What's to want? I have my family close by. My ranch. My land. My peace and quiet. A simple, uncomplicated life." He left out the small detail that Bill was trying to sell the one piece of it that Wade treasured most.

"Hmm."

Something about her drawn brows prompted him to pry, even though he shouldn't. "You don't like your reality?"

Trish nodded forward so they'd keep walking. They weren't far from the clearing now. "I don't have some ritzy, glamorous life." She waved her hand. "I work in a cubicle with gray walls and no window. Each morning I have to remind myself I need to pay my rent in order to get out of bed to go."

"That sounds miserable."

"When I went to college, I thought it was important to be practical. Get a degree that would guarantee me a job. Creative writing was only an elective back then. My best friend tried to talk me into changing my major to English lit, but I was too afraid, I guess." There was sadness in her tone. Defeat. His heart pulled at the pain he heard there.

"Afraid of what?"

"I'm all I've got. If I mess that up . . ."

"No family?"

"Uh . . .no." Her answer seemed hesitant, as though the topic might strike a chord she didn't want to hear. "I wish I had a family like yours. They seem really wonderful."

"We're a little dysfunctional," Wade replied with a light laugh. "But I wouldn't change them for the world." Well, except Uncle Bill's constant draw, trying to earn a quick buck off a ranch he'd never really appreciated. "You write to escape?"

Trish shrugged. "Yeah."

"Watch your step." One large tree root blocked the path that marked the entry to the clearing. Once on flat ground, bathed in moonlight, he dropped Trish's hand and busied himself pulling one of the two blankets Grams had packed, and spread it on the ground.

"It's so beautiful out here." It wasn't until Trish settled onto the blanket, long legs outstretched and crossed at the ankles, that Wade noticed how small it was. Had Grams done this on purpose? "I know I keep saying that, but I really mean it. I've never been anywhere quite like this."

He unfolded the second blanket, about to spread it next to the first one. But a shiver hit Trish so violently that her whole body shook. "Here." He offered the second one to her.

"Surely someone's excited about your writing?" He guessed it wasn't that Howie fellow.

"My best friend, Mindy." A gentle smile fell across the lips all too prominent in the moonlight. "She's the one who threw me the I-finished-a-book party back at home. And actually, she gifted me this retreat as a congratulatory present."

"Generous friend."

"She's like a sister."

A little further digging in the backpack revealed a couple of mini wine cooler bottles. Wade shook his head at Grams. Maybe she had ulterior motives after all. Least she could have done was pack him a beer. "Want some fruity drink?" He lightly tossed a bottle to Trish. "It's a twist-off."

"Thanks."

Wade tried to ignore Trish bundled in a blanket, but it was cute. With just her head and hands poking out of the dark blue fleece, he busied himself gathering firewood after discovering the lighter in the backpack. *Grams thought of everything.*

"Where are your parents?" Trish asked, her voice

quieter now than it had been. She must have known it was a delicate question.

He could shut her down again, change the subject. Instead, with a deep breath, he lit the fire he'd built. "Up there." He pointed toward the stars. "They passed away when I was really young." Wade couldn't bring himself to tell her the details.

"I'm so sorry, Wade. I'm sure they were wonderful people."

"The best." It touched him how Trish automatically assumed the best of his parents when she hadn't even claimed any of her own. He wanted to ask more about that, but it seemed too personal a topic. With the fire roaring, Wade eased onto the much too small blanket. Shadow had laid her claim to a bottom corner, forcing him to sit even closer to Trish.

They sat in silence a while, both gazing at the stars. Galaxies floated overhead. Wade stated, "Willing to bet you don't see stars like this in Omaha."

"This is a great spot," she finally said after a sip of her drink.

"We used to camp out here when I was younger. Me and my cousins." He smiled at the memories of them pitching a tent, then leaving it empty all night to sleep out under the stars. "Little tip—that stream does *not* have the best fish . . . but we caught some anyway. Allen was the survivalist, determined we wouldn't go begging for scraps at the house."

"Especially not fancy-smancy s'mores, I bet." Trish tipped the little bottle up, emptying it. He offered her the second one, and she accepted. He wouldn't drink it anyway.

Wade nudged her. "Hey now, I tried them your way. I admitted I was wrong."

"You ever been anywhere outside of Wyoming?" Trish asked. "College doesn't count since that was in the same state."

"Of course." Wade tried to adjust himself on the blanket, but everything he tried had him leaning against Trish. After three attempts, he gave in. *It didn't mean anything*, he reminded himself. It was all for writing inspiration and he had to make sure the predators didn't take too much interest in her. "California one summer to visit cousins. Cancun for a wedding. Alaska with Allen on a fishing trip."

"Wow, you *do* get out!" She was definitely flirting with him now. It had to be the wine cooler, allowing her to let her guard down. "Yet, you chose to stay here?" It didn't sound like an insult, just a casual question.

"Look around," Wade said, trying to keep his eyes off her. The scent of her shampoo—something flowery like lilac—drifted to him on the night's breeze. Trish shivered, and he had to fight the urge to put his arm around her. "This land is special. I could never leave it behind, not for the winning lottery ticket."

"You're lucky, you know that?" Trish leaned her head on his shoulder, as if it were the most casual thing in the word. Wade found he couldn't breathe. Couldn't move.

"Why's that?"

"You've always known where your home is. You've always known where you belong." She shivered again, and this time Wade couldn't help himself. His arm eased around her back and pulled her a little closer. She snuggled in against him. Firelight reflected in those soft eyes. Her lips were close enough to kiss.

"You don't feel like you belong in Omaha?" Could she feel the crazy thumping of his heart? Surely it was hammering against her cheek.

"I've never felt like I belonged anywhere I lived. But being out here . . . It's probably that it's a romance writers' retreat, the whole fantasy element and all that. But it feels the closest to home I've ever been. I can't explain it."

"You could see yourself living on a ranch?" He shouldn't go there. It was better not to let such fantasies take flight. But he found himself waiting breathlessly for her answer, his eyes drawn to those soft lips. What would happen if he kissed her?

"Are you kidding? All the books I could write out here, especially by that fireplace. You'd never get me to leave!" The small wine cooler in her hand reminded him a kiss was a bad idea. She wasn't drunk or slurring her words, but she was certainly more animated and open than she'd been with him. Surely the drink had helped her drop her guard. And she hadn't mentioned that Hank fellow once.

He could see the allure of falling. It probably felt a little like flying. Maybe in another time, another life, he could fall for Trish Meadows. But the downfall was too great a risk. How did you continue flying if you lost the one you loved? Too many nights Grams had sobbed herself to sleep. Too many times he'd caught her in the living room gripping their last anniversary photo, tears silently sliding down her cheeks. She'd lost too much weight, unable to eat for weeks.

If Trish loved it out here so much, why would she ever choose a city? "Why Omaha?"

"Mindy." She tipped the tiny bottle up again, and he couldn't seem to stop staring at her lips. *Did they taste like the cherry wine cooler?* "She was my neighbor when I was fifteen, when I lived with a family in Nebraska. It was the first time in my life that I ever made a real friend."

Shadow perked up at a twig snapping in the distance, but Trish didn't seem to notice as she continued. "It was the best year, but then I moved. We vowed to meet back up at college. Be roommates and all that. I would have gone to any school to have her back in my life. She's like a sister. The only one I've ever had."

Wade's heart ached at the sadness laced in her words. At the things she wasn't telling him. He wanted desperately to know everything there was to know about Trish, but he couldn't bring himself to ask. He couldn't let things go there. "Did she major in business, too?"

He felt Trish shake her head against his shoulder. "She's a computer geek to the core. For me, business felt safe. I was always good with numbers."

"You're good with words, too." When she pulled back and stared at him, he swallowed. Firelight illuminated her eyes, making his stomach flutter in an odd way. "I mean, I'm guessing you are. I haven't read any—"

With a sudden pounce, Trish stopped him. Her lips crushed against his, and for a moment Wade was dazed, unsure how it happened. His lips responded within seconds, unable to do anything but yield to her kiss's allure. He had enough awareness to note her lips did in fact taste like cherry before the kiss deepened. He should pull away, should stop himself before he fell over the edge.

But Trish was the first to pull back, a sheepish smile on her face. She started to say something, but he kissed her forehead instead. Words wouldn't do either of them a lot of good right now. Tomorrow, he'd have to straighten things out. But for tonight . . .

he slid down on the blanket till he lay flat and opened an arm to her.

Without hesitation, she curled against him and nestled her head into his chest.

"The fire'll burn a couple of hours longer." Wade liked this. Just as it was. "No harm enjoying the stars for a little while longer."

Trish murmured, "Um-hmm."

Tomorrow, he'd reinforce those walls to protect his heart. But tonight, he wanted to pretend that the woman he held in his arms could stay there forever.

CHAPTER 11

SOMETHING FURRY BRUSHED against her arm, and Trish shot up. She was disoriented and felt a slight pounding in her head. "Hey, Shadow." At the mention of her name, the pup leapt up closer to her pillow, and stared with a tilted head, heartily wagging her tail.

The cushion of her mattress and the lilac curtains brought her to the reality that this was her room. The memory from last night—being wrapped in a blanket and leaning against Wade—made her cheeks redden. She *kissed* him! She blamed the wine cooler. She would've never done that if she hadn't been so relaxed. Falling for Wade . . . it was some silly fantasy. In a few days, she'd head back to Omaha, never to see him again. How long would it take before he forgot her completely? A couple of months? Weeks?

Trish tossed the covers off her legs and rushed to the writing table for her phone, relieved to find it was barely seven. She feared she'd missed her breakfast date, though Wade hadn't been shy about waking her before.

How had she gotten back to her room? She didn't remember walking through the woods, even groggily. Surely Wade hadn't carried her the entire way on that dark, uneven trail.

Shadow hopped off the bed, ears perked with interest. Perhaps she thought they were going on an adventure, now that she was standing and running her hands through her hair. "How did *you* end up here?" she asked, but Shadow just watched her with that goofy smile, tongue lolling.

Next to her phone sat a rolled-up extension cord. Trish nearly squealed with glee. She could write for half an hour before she absolutely had to rinse off in the shower. She plugged in the cord and strung it toward her laptop on her bed. Shadow sprawled out on the rug beside her as Trish typed away.

"How would you feel about having breakfast in

town with me? You'll like Mable's." Kate asked when Trish was halfway down the stairs, Shadow racing by. The loyal dog had curled up on a rug outside the bathroom door until Trish finished showering.

"Mable's sounds great." Trish wanted to ask where Wade was but didn't want to be rude. "I'm starving." The other writers, she knew from her itinerary, had scheduled writing blocks this morning. Glenda had mentioned something about a special breakfast delivery right to their cabins.

"Wade had to take care of a few things on the ranch this morning," Kate explained. Her hands rubbed her belly, and a momentary wince of pain crossed her face. "So I told him I'd fill in. I'm no cowboy, but I promise I'm a lot more fun."

"I'm sure you're more cheerful," Trish added. "You sure you're up to the trip, though?"

"Oh, yes. Just Braxton Hicks." Kate waved a hand in dismissal. "I'll have you drive the truck, though. It's getting harder to fit behind the steering wheel these days."

Trish didn't think it necessary to admit she'd never driven a truck. Surely it couldn't be that different than a car. Probably less chance of getting stuck in the mud. "Of course."

"C'mon, Shadow. Your daddy left you all alone today, so you're coming with us." Kate must have noticed Trish's quizzical expression. "Mable's has a dog-friendly patio. Figured it was too beautiful a morning to sit inside anyway. We don't have too many of these left before winter, you know."

Trish had a vision of the truck Lina drove, but it certainly wasn't the monstrosity that sat in the driveway. "Is that a diesel?"

"Grams always wanted a big truck," Kate said, pulling the passenger door open. Shadow hopped in and made her way to the back seat, obviously familiar with this routine. "You might need to give me a shove inside."

"We can eat here at the ranch if it's easier," Trish said, feeling guilty about Kate babysitting her. *Isn't this part of Wade's chaperone package?* "I don't mind."

"Nonsense. I need out! I've been cooped up in that house almost a week." Trish helped Kate into the truck and shut the door behind her. "Besides, I have a job in town later. House I need to photograph."

She climbed into the driver's seat. "I feel like I'm about to drive a tank," Trish said. "You sure you trust me?" What if she broke an axel with the next pothole? Her savings would be drained forking over money for a repair like that. "We could take my car instead."

"Your car is cute, but I won't fit. Trust me."

Trish navigated carefully through the winding dirt driveway until they met the gravel road. From what she remembered, the town of Starlight was two miles to the east, behind one of the big rolling hills. "When's your husband due back?"

"Should be home in a week. It'll be so nice to sleep in my own bed again."

"You don't live out at the ranch?"

"Haven't since I got married." Kate shook her head, another wince flashing across her face. It was gone as quickly as it appeared. Didn't keep Trish from feeling a little nervous, though. *What if Kate goes into labor?* "Ty and I have a house in town, right on the edge. Big yard. Small pasture for a couple of horses we want once Ty retires from the military for good."

Trish caught a glimpse of a dreamy look in Kate's eyes. Had she ever had that look about Henry? She didn't think so.

"So, is it just Wade and your grandma?"

"Allen and Chet's parents live there too, when they're home. Aunt Tabby's a motivational speaker. She's picked up a lot of recent popularity. They're in Europe while she's on tour." Kate dug through her purse until she pulled out a pink-cased cell phone. She skittered a text with her quick fingers. "I think it's hard for Grams to have such a quiet house. That's why I've been staying out there a lot while Ty's gone. This retreat, it's good for her."

In a couple of miles, they crested the rolling hill and at the base sat the town of Starlight. It didn't look like much from up here. Someone had said something about twelve thousand people. Quite the change from Omaha, but it reminded Trish of the smaller towns she'd lived in. Some much smaller than Starlight.

"You live here all your life?" Trish asked.

"Yep, except a couple of years that I dabbled with photography classes in college. It's home, you know?"

Trish didn't know how to say she didn't, so she just smiled.

"Take a right at the stop sign. Mable's is three blocks down from there, on the corner. Can't miss the big red sign." Kate typed out another text, this one longer than the first. "If you're into pancakes, Mable makes the best in Wyoming."

Trish found a parking spot not too far from the door, despite the number of cars parked along the street. She didn't want Kate to have to walk far. "I'm afraid you'll have to let me and Shadow both out."

They found a small table in the patio's remote corner, which was perfectly fine with Trish. She'd grown so used to the solitude on the ranch that she wasn't eager to be in the middle of a crowd. After they placed their pancake order, Kate jumped right in with a blunt question. "So, what's up with you and this Henry guy? All the other writing gals talk about him, and I can't say any of them sound like fans."

"Recent ex-boyfriend." Trish stirred three packets of caramel creamer into her coffee. The sweeter the better this morning. "We dated for about six months. Really thought we were on track to get engaged. Married someday."

"Rumor has it he's not a fan of you becoming a romance author."

Trish tapped her spoon gently against her mug before setting it on a napkin. "That's one way to put it." She took a cautious sip until she was sure her coffee wasn't too hot.

"Do you love him?"

Nearly choking, Trish set the mug down and rested her hands in her lap. It was going to be a long day if coffee betrayed her. Shadow came to her rescue then, her chin resting in Trish's lap. "What's that?"

"A simple question," Kate said. "You either love the guy or you don't."

The question felt like a trap, but Trish couldn't pin down why. "I thought I did." She rubbed Shadow behind the ears. "Thought I could anyway." The realization created a weird twisting in her chest, as if she'd just discovered a lie.

"So, no then."

Two plates of pancakes slid onto their table, along with a variety rack of syrups. Trish found herself drawn to the strawberry and almost laughed. Would Wade think she was being too fancy if she used strawberry instead of good old maple syrup?

"What would you do?" Kate continued,

spreading butter on her pancakes. "If he begged you to take him back? Would you do it?"

Maybe this breakfast had a little less to do with filling in for a busy cowboy and a little more to do with interrogation. Trish felt practically naked across the table from Kate's assessing eyes.

She knew the answer Kate was looking for, and she suspected it was because of Wade. She couldn't remember who was older, but Kate was sure acting like the overprotective big sister. Did she know about their kiss? "I thought that was what I wanted, even though everyone told me I was better off without him. But after some distance . . ." And a certain kiss that left her toes curled hours later . . .

"Change can be scary," Kate said in a way that was less overprotective big sister and more compassionate friend. "Sometimes it's easier to stay miserable because it's familiar. Comfortable in an odd sort of way." Kate's fork circled over her pancakes. "Take my brother, for instance."

Trish perked up at the mention of Wade, curious what his sister might divulge, yet not wanting to appear eager for information. "Wade?"

"He's convinced he wants to be alone. It's what he's used to, so he doesn't give anything better a chance." Kate stuffed in a forkful of pancake, her eyes closing in delight. Once she swallowed, she added, "You're already doing something brave, Trish."

"I am?" Trish felt about as far from brave as it got.

"Chasing your dream of being a writer. Most people would stick to their nine-to-five no matter how much they hate it because they're afraid to take a chance. But you're here. That counts for something."

"You're pretty good at boosting egos," Trish said. She slipped a scrap of bacon under the table. She'd seen Wade share a graham cracker the other night and figured bacon couldn't be off limits. Shadow rewarded her with a lick to her fingers. "Why does Wade want to be alone?" The question might be too bold, but she didn't think Wade would ever tell her himself.

Kate seemed to size her up, to decide how to respond. She took her time finishing another bite and taking a drink of her water. "Our parents died when we were young. Really bad car accident. Dad died instantly. Mom was in intensive care for a week, but she didn't make it."

"That's so horrible. I'm sorry." She had dreamed what it would be like to have both parents in her life, but to lose them at the same time . . .

"Grams told Wade that our mom died of a broken heart. He was five, but I don't think that ever left him. Then our grandpa passed last year, and Grams has had a really hard time with it. Wade's been there to hold her when she falls apart, and I think it's got him afraid." Kate pointed her fork at Trish. "You're not allowed to tell him I told you any of this."

Trish promised not to say a word.

"Wade's also seen me fall apart several times since Ty has been gone. It's stressful enough that he's in a war zone, but add in all these extra hormones . . ."

"I'd give anything to *have* a family." Trish poked around at her pancake, her appetite not quite what it was. "I can't imagine what it must be like, to lose them."

"Well, this week, you're part of *our* family." Kate raised her water glass in toast. "We're happy to have you here. Happier that you're forcing Wade out of his comfort zone, even if it *is* at Grams' insistence."

BETSY'S BOOT Boutique sat across the street from Mable's. Kate must've seen Trish eyeing their sign with longing when they left Mable's, because she insisted they go inside. "But Shadow—"

"Betsy loves Shadow. Always has treats behind the counter for her." Shadow's tail wagged in eager confirmation as they crossed the street. "Are you prepared to spend the money?" Kate asked. "These aren't your typical fashion boots. They're made with the intent to be worn. Worked in."

Trish nodded. She'd fallen in love with the boots

Kate loaned her, but she'd have to give them back. "I really miss being around horses. I think a good pair of boots might serve as a reminder not to put off finding a way to be around them more." Someday, she might have one of her own.

Kate clapped her hands together, a bright smile on her face. "Let's get you going. You'll be a cowgirl in no time. I have the perfect pair in mind!"

CHAPTER 12

 *ade*

WADE HAD SPENT the better part of the morning hiding away in his cabin, refinishing kitchen cabinet doors. He'd made a couple of checks on the herds and knocked out a few chores, but Allen and Chet weren't counting on his help today or tomorrow. In fact, Grams had lined up some high school kid to help out, freeing him up.

The fear of her wrath for skipping out on his chaperone duties this morning kept him safely tucked inside his cabin. That, and the thought of encountering Trish so soon after that kiss . . . He just couldn't. He'd already bribed Kate to take her into town for breakfast and buy him the morning.

His gray-striped cat squeezed in through the window he'd left cracked open and plodded onto the floor. Squirrel scanned the room for Shadow, but with the dog missing, found his way to Wade. "Hey there, buddy," Wade said to the cat. "Brought you some milk."

Shadow, the traitor, had followed Wade upstairs as he carried a passed-out Trish to her bed the previous night. Before he slipped off her boots, his dog curled up on the end of Trish's bed and fell asleep. This morning, he left her there.

With wood conditioner drying on the last two cabinet doors, Wade slipped off his latex gloves. He retrieved a plastic bowl he'd filled with milk before anyone in the house awoke.

Sleep had all but eluded Wade last night. Though he'd been exhausted from a long day, he tossed and turned at the memory of Trish in his arms, and her soft snoring. It was oddly perfect, and that bothered him more than anything. Even more than the riveting kiss they shared. One he should never have let happen.

As Squirrel lapped up the milk, Wade stepped back against the window to assess his progress on the kitchen area, desperate for a distraction to his troubled thoughts. The cabin had started as one open room. Wade moved into what was once a cramped kitchenette and reached for the can of stain under the sink. With the additional cabinet he'd added, along with the island able to serve four, the space felt expanded. Open.

Wade stared out at the rest of the room.

He was glad to be rid of the two sets of bunks and the worn-out olive couch that had sat beneath the big window for as long as he could remember. "Need to get something new," he told Squirrel. The cat flicked his tail but didn't offer any ideas on how to fill the empty living space. He bet Trish would have some opinions. But Wade quickly pushed that thought aside. "Maybe a pull-out couch?" Wade had broken down the frame of the bunks, using most of it as kindling. The shoddy couch had been hauled to the dump.

Removing the lid from the can of stain, Wade pulled on another pair of latex gloves.

Though he planned for it to be just him, he didn't like the idea of sleeping in his living room and kitchen. "What do you think, Squirrel? Do I need to build another room?" Squirrel just blinked at him. He'd never taken on a project as massive as an addition. Wade had a buddy in town who might be willing to help him. But if Uncle Bill somehow convinced Grams she needed the money, an addition would be a foolish dream at best.

Dipping his brush into the stain, Wade spent the rest of the morning coating the doors and the insides of the cabinets while his cat took to lounging in the sun.

He stopped only when he ran out of stain. The work had been good to keep away the rampant thoughts about the alluring writer. If he avoided the house for a couple of days and kept busy on his cabin, maybe things could quiet back down to the way they used to be.

Wade laughed out loud at that stupidity. Grams would have his hide if he ducked out on his chaperone duties. It'd been years since she'd been out to the cabin in the north pasture, but he'd bet the ranch she'd track him down by sundown if he didn't head back soon.

After cleaning up what he could, he reluctantly decided to head back. Maybe after a quick appearance at the house, he could slip away into town. He needed to run to the hardware store for another can of stain.

"Sorry, Squirrel," he said to the lounging cat. The poor guy looked positively bored without Shadow to tease. "Gotta run." Wade picked him up and gave the sleepy Squirrel a good long belly rub; the cat responded by purring—till Wade dropped him onto the front deck.

Wade locked the door behind him. For years, the cabin had never been locked. It was tucked away and not easy to access. It hadn't been used in almost three years, since the last time wolves were an issue around their property. But now that Wade was fixing it up, he didn't want anyone breaking in.

Sinking money into it was more like it if Grams ever took Bill's idea to heart. His uncle had never appreciated the ranch the way his grandpa had. The way Wade still did.

Without Shadow on the back of his ATV, Wade hightailed it back to the house, more afraid of Grams' fury than facing Trish in the light of day. He wondered how much she remembered. She hadn't been anything more than a little tipsy, but she'd certainly been tired. The best thing he could do, he decided, was pull her aside first chance he had and establish that they could be friends. Nothing more.

Satisfied with his plan, Wade slipped in through the kitchen door expecting an entourage to greet him. But the house was very quiet. His heart rate increased in slight panic. Had Kate gone into labor? Wade had purposely left his phone on his night-stand, but now he regretted it.

He strode into the living room, finding that empty as well. He'd best grab his phone and find out what he missed. But a few feet from the staircase, he heard a voice and stopped. The door to the office tucked under the stairs was open a few inches.

"He offered *how* much?"

Wade ran both hands over the back of his neck. Grams. Talking to Uncle Bill. *Should've warned her.*

"That's an awful lot of money, Bill." Wade couldn't discern from her response what that meant. *Is she considering it?*

From where he stood, frozen, he could see a picture of Grandpa on the fireplace mantel, decked out in his favorite hat and a belt buckle that'd been passed down from *his* grandpa. A buckle Wade kept in a drawer but was afraid to mess up by wearing. What would he think of all this?

"I need time to think about it," Grams said.

Wade's heart thudded in his chest. He'd hoped she would just say no outright.

"I hear what you're saying, Bill, believe me, I do. But you know I never make impulsive decisions. Give me some time—" A huffed sigh sounded from the room. "Fine, if he needs an answer that quick, I'll get one by then. Good-bye, Bill."

Feeling as though he'd been eavesdropping, Wade panicked. Should he wait and confront Grams? Would she be upset that he hadn't told her Bill called? It was the realization that his fists were balled at his sides that sent him away. His grandpa always taught him to make sure he was in his calmest state if he wanted to have a rational conversation about irrational things.

Wade was supposed to take part in some lasso demonstration soon, but he felt too upset to be around people. He'd text Kate, beg another favor from her to cover for him. An afternoon drive through the Bighorn mountains might calm him.

Rounding the house, Wade went to fish his keys out of his pocket but came up empty. He'd left them in the stable that morning when he swung through. He hoped he could slip in and out without his cousins noticing him. The last thing he needed was Allen trying to rile him up about his moonlit walk.

Careful to close the stable door gently when he entered, Wade poked his head forward in search of anyone who might delay his getaway. When he didn't see Allen, Chet, or any high school kid, he took a couple of steps forward.

"—name was Scooby. You know, like the dog on that cartoon." He'd still know that soft voice weeks after she left. "I think you would've liked him. Had a personality as big as the state of Wyoming and liked to walk me into tree branches, too."

Who is Trish talking to? A couple more steps forward, and Wade caught the flash of something shiny from a pair of boots inside a stall. The closer he came, the more he could see Trish filling out a new pair of cowgirl boots. Of course she found a pair with something sparkly on them. Tight jeans complemented those legs, and his eyes traveled to a horse brush in her hand.

"Oh, hey," she said, her cheeks instantly turning red. "Didn't hear you."

"Telling Daphne stories?" He tried to tease, but the words were hard enough to form on their own. In that cute striped button-up shirt and hair half pulled back in a stubby ponytail, Trish looked positively at home.

"She likes my stories."

"Come here often, do you?"

Trish resumed brushing. "I may have snuck in here a time or two, haven't I, Daphne?" The horse nudged her gently, exceedingly happy for the extra attention. "Until we went riding, I'd forgotten how much I miss being around horses. Of course, I had to add a horse into my work in progress."

There were things he needed to say to Trish, but he couldn't remember a single one right now. If ever there were a perfect match for him, surely it was the woman standing on the other side of the stall talking to her horse. Why did fate insist on torturing him? "Let me get you a different brush. There's one Daphne likes best."

And there were his keys, on the ledge next to the horse brushes. Wade reached for them, then stopped. After his absence so far, Grams would spontaneously combust if he snuck away. But he could stay out here with Trish, let the tension of Bill's phone call settle, and appease Grams at the same time.

"Here." He held the brush out to Trish.

"Trade you." As she handed him the one she'd used, their hands grazed and both brushes wobbled in the unsteady handoff. They each scrambled, but the brushes dropped and their hands tangled together. The heat of her touch ignited a place inside him that Wade had always considered dormant.

"S-sorry," she stammered.

Wade yanked his hands away and instantly bent down to pick up the brushes. "It's my fault." He dropped Daphne's favorite brush into Trish's cupped hands, careful to avoid contact this time. "I-I think we should talk." It came out deeper than he intended. But it was best to get the hard conversation out of the way. "About last night." Before she made too many assumptions.

Ducking her head, she agreed. "Yeah, we probably should."

"Look, I think it's best if we keep this thing between us as friends."

"Friends." Was she agreeing or disappointed?

"You're not staying, and I'm not—"

"There you two are!" Grams burst in through the side door. "We've been searching the property for the likes of you."

"Grams—"

"You two are going to miss the roping demonstration. I already convinced Allen to take over, but everyone is waiting on you 'fore we start." She winked at Wade before she strode toward the door, leaving him with his jaw half-open.

"You can come back after," he told Trish. "Now you know which brush Daphne likes best."

Trish rubbed Daphne against her neck and planted a kiss on her muzzle. "I'll come back later. Promise." She slipped out of the stall, completely unapologetic for such a show of affection for a horse that wasn't even her own. As if it were the most natural thing in the world.

"Come on, you two. Scoot!" Seemed Grams wasn't going to leave the stable unless they followed.

Wade found it harder to picture this wonder of a woman living in a crowded, noisy city. The problem was, it was becoming much too easy to picture her living on a Wyoming ranch.

 rish

Trish let out a yawn the next morning as she took a seat at the dining table for the writers' daily brainstorming session. She'd missed as many as she made with the special itinerary Lina created for her, but today she was looking forward to losing herself in a conversation about fictional characters.

Several sets of eyes assessed her curiously, and Trish avoided their stares by reaching to the center of the table for a cherry scone.

"Someone stay out too late with a certain cowboy?" Glenda nudged her with her elbow, eyebrows raised in suggestion.

"What?" Trish fought another yawn but managed to shake her head.

"You didn't sit outside by the fire pit or take another romantic walk in the moonlight?" Lizzie chimed in, evident disappointment in her tone.

"After that lasso demonstration thing, I spent the rest of the time writing. I wrote three chapters!" She looked around the table, expecting cheers of excitement. Instead, they all seemed a little underwhelmed. Like maybe she mentioned a tuna sandwich she had for lunch. "Over six thousand words. It's my best day so far."

"Inspired by anyone we know?" Marti rolled up the sleeves of her running jacket and reached for a glass of ice water in front of her. She was the only one drinking water. The rest were sipping on mimosas.

"And please tell us it's not that boring guy from *Omaha*," the fourth writer added. Trish felt bad that she couldn't remember her name without consulting her itinerary. "The auditor. He's such a—"

"Dud," Marti said.

"Yes, a dud."

"But that cowboy fella, on the other hand," Glenda said. "Seems like you two are spending a lot of time together."

Trish's cheeks had to be the color the apples. She focused on the wire basket at the center of the table. How had this turned into a spotlight on her love life?

One that was a fantasy at best. Sure, that kiss had spun her world sideways and still gave her butterflies at its memory, *but sheesh!* It wasn't as if it'd happen again. Wade had made it pretty clear in the stable: they needed to stay friends.

The days were ticking away, and soon Trish would go back to her reality. "It's what I signed up for," Trish said, though she knew her argument was a weak one. Technically *she* hadn't even signed herself up. That had been Mindy's handiwork.

"But he's single," Lizzie said. "You're single."

"Only recently," Trish reminded. "And I don't live here, remember? Can we please talk about our stories? I really need help with a road block. I stranded my characters in a rainstorm while they were on a horseback riding adventure, ten miles from the ranch. What do I do with that?"

"Oh!" Glenda rubbed her hands together, her eyes lighting up. "I think we can come up with a few ideas."

Trish let out a small sigh of relief that the writers seemed content to leave her non-existent relationship with Wade alone in exchange for some plot talk.

"No!" Trish tried the power button again, then pulled the cord out of her laptop and stuck it back in. She checked the outlet to make sure the plug was secure. Then she proceeded to unplug her lamp to try her power cord there.

But after a full day of writing, The Dinosaur was dead.

She yanked the plug out of the wall and lugged her heavy laptop downstairs. She plugged it in by the recliner and, hoping, hit the power button

Nothing.

She sat on the arm of the recliner, The Dinosaur in her lap, and curled her fingers around its thick edges.

Her only saving grace was the number of times she'd hit save on her thumb drive. Most people didn't even use them anymore. But Trish had never left home without one. She knew this day would come, but she'd hoped it might be a couple of years away yet. She wasn't ready to part with the one prized possession she owned.

Henry had always scoffed at her ancient laptop. His snide comment about serious writers investing in better equipment came back to her then, and she found herself boiling with irritation.

"You okay?"

Had she been too preoccupied to hear Wade's approaching steps? "The Dinosaur is dead."

"Come again?"

"My laptop." Trish let out a deep breath. She hadn't seen him all day, and she didn't realize until now that she missed him and his sarcastic remarks. "I call it The Dinosaur because it's so old and bulky. Fitting term of endearment. It's dead." Were tears forming at the corners of her eyes? She turned away from Wade and busied herself with gathering up and winding the cord.

"The battery died?"

Trish shook her head and squeezed her eyes shut. "Nope." A tear splashed against the hard cover.

"There's a shop in Gillette," Wade suggested. "I think they close at six. But if we left soon we could catch them. Mike does all our computer work for the ranch. You may have noticed we don't exactly have state-of-the-art computers out here."

Was he really offering to drive her to another town to get her problem fixed? *Why would he do that?* "How far's Gillette?"

"An hour, max. Can you give me twenty minutes? I need to grab a shower. I won't force you to ride with me after a day's work. That's a special kind of torture I reserve for my cousins. Or my sister when she's being particularly irritating."

She swiped away a tear, hoping he didn't notice. "Thank you."

"Hey." He was somehow closer now, though Trish hadn't heard him take a step. "It'll be okay." He reached out a hand to her and helped her to her feet. "If anyone can fix it, Mike can."

"What if he can't?" Dang it, she was going to cry.

A firm hand cupped her shoulder, and Wade

waited for her to look him in the eyes. He didn't make her feel guilty for her tears the way Henry usually did. "We'll cross that bridge if we come to it, okay?"

"Okay." She very much wanted to curl up against him, feel his arms wrapped around her, ranch smell or not. But friends didn't do that kind of thing. Instead, she took a step back toward the staircase and practically ran away from the man who kept surprising her in the most unexpected ways.

She leaned against her closed door once upstairs and let out a big breath. Henry would never have offered to take her ten minutes across town for her laptop, much less an hour away. She could just hear him now. *I told you to get a new one. Are you surprised your ancient one died?"*

In a desperate attempt to push all thoughts of Wade from her mind, she yanked her cell phone off her nightstand and dialed Mindy. "How did you never tell me what a dud Henry was?"

"Oh, sweetie," Mindy said, not at all put off by the abrupt greeting. Had she been expecting this eventual outburst? "I tried once. But you defended him with every excuse in the book."

"You should've tried harder!"

"Sometimes you have to realize those things for yourself."

Emotions twisted inside Trish. She'd hoped by being here, she could prove to Henry that she was a serious writer. That her dream was worthy of recognition. Why had she been fighting so hard? If Henry loved her, he would have encouraged her no matter what. "I guess you're right."

"He isn't a terrible guy," Mindy admitted. "Just not the greatest guy. Not *your* guy, Trish."

"What did I see in him?"

"A safe choice," Mindy replied without missing a beat, as if she'd been saving that answer for weeks. "But Trish, you deserve so much more than he can offer you."

"So I've been told," she muttered.

THEIR RIDE to Gillette was a quiet if bumpy one. Trish couldn't stop thoughts from racing through her mind. What did she really have to go back to in Omaha? A dinky, overpriced apartment, a job she didn't love? One best friend who was swamped with her new IT business? Trish didn't even have a goldfish.

But Starlight . . . it wasn't hers for the taking. It was a dream, one that Lina had done very well creating, for some enthusiastic romance writers.

No matter how she looked at things, though, Trish felt as though something had to change. Henry believed you had to work long hours to impress the right people and climb to the top. And for him, it seemed to be working. A month ago, he'd been promoted to a senior auditor.

Yet, Trish was still the lowly cubicle worker on the bottom of the totem pole, and not a bit sad about not climbing that corporate ladder. She'd always known, somewhere deep down, that there had to be more to life than just getting by. Something that didn't involve long nights and weekends sacrificed for someone else's dream.

"You seem deep in thought," Wade said as they passed the Gillette sign welcoming them into town.

"You ever feel you got stuck in a rut and didn't even know it?" she asked.

Wade slowed the truck for a stoplight. "Can't say I have."

"My life. I just don't know how I got here." What if she had been brave enough to change her major after that creative writing class? What if she'd been willing to take a risky chance? Maybe she could have had twelve novels published by now, too. "Did you know that I can't even have a grill at my apartment?"

"Well that's just tragic."

"Right? And if I tried to light a fire pit on my coat-closet-sized balcony, I'd be evicted before the fire department showed up to put it out." Trish crossed and uncrossed her ankles. Was her dream of a permanent home so big that she was willing to sacrifice happiness for that stability?

Wade steered the truck around a curve, slowing

for a turn into a small parking lot. "Maybe you should move." Wade cleared his throat, and added, "You know, like to a small house or something. Apartments seem so confining."

"Yeah, maybe." But her lease wasn't up for eight months yet. The One-Man Tech Shop, Trish read. "Please tell me more than one guy works here."

"Nope." Wade pushed open his door. "You read the sign."

Trish groaned, afraid all hope was lost for The Dinosaur if her fate rested in the hands of one man. That was one perk for Omaha, she had to admit. When Mindy wasn't an option, she had no shortage of computer repair shops at her disposal each time The Dinosaur acted up. If one couldn't fix the issue, usually another could.

"Hey, Mike," Wade called out once they were both in the store.

Trish hugged her laptop as though she were bringing it to have it put down, even though it likely put itself down hours ago. She followed Wade to the front counter. She had a lot of error messages and blue screens before, but never a completely unresponsive computer.

"What do we got here?" Mike asked after he and Wade exchanged some small talk about business and the ranch. Trish tried to follow, but her concentration was lost to the reality that there might be no hope. "Wow, this is one of the oldest models I've seen in a while."

"Oh, come on," Wade said. "Grams has an older one than this."

Mike shook his head, his glasses sliding with it. He pushed them up the bridge of his nose. "Nope. This is about ten years old, right?" he directed toward Trish.

A tiny bubble of hope soared. "Yes." Trish briefly explained what had happened earlier in the day, then went into more detail about the battery life depleting within minutes. The more she talked about the issues, the more she realized how many there were. Signs for months that things were headed for doom.

Kind of like her recent relationship.

That revelation stopped her midsentence.

"I'm not sure there's much I can do for it," Mike admitted. He hooked up a tester to the power cord. "This still appears to work—at half capacity, but it's functioning." He performed a few more tests on the laptop itself, but nothing seemed to suggest signs of life.

"I think it's a goner," Wade said to Trish as delicately as he might have told her a pet goldfish had died.

"I could keep it for a couple days," Mike offered. "Take it apart. See if I can revive it."

"No," Trish said, a firm conviction in her voice.

"I think it's time to cut my losses." Her laptop, the one almost new possession she'd worked three jobs her first year in college to afford, had been more than good to her. She'd written countless stories that would never see the light of day, and one or two that with any luck just might. "I saved everything important on a thumb drive, except for a few hundred words." She gathered The Dinosaur in her arms, hugging it against her chest.

"I would offer to buy it for parts," Mike said. "But frankly, I think most of it's fried. I could dispose of it for you."

Trish shook her head. "Thank you, but I'll take it with me." She wasn't sure what she was going to do with The Dinosaur, but tossing it away at a strange store like a cheap piece of scrap metal didn't quite seem right. Maybe it would make a nice door stop. Or self-defense weapon.

"What are you going to do?" Wade asked when they were back in the truck.

"Buy a new one." Trish took in a deep breath and let it out. Earlier this week, the old Trish would have been sobbing into her laptop in despair. But this newly emerging Trish was able to let go more easily. To look forward to new possibilities. "Are there any stores in town that sell laptops?" She'd never owned a brand-new one before. The very thought made her giddy.

"I know a place close by."

"Yeah?"

"Let's get you a new computer. Maybe one a little lighter than your former . . ."

"Cement block?"

"I can't believe that thing didn't crush your legs on the drive down."

Trish had to admit she had trouble with the idea of letting The Dinosaur go. It'd been such a consistent part of her life. Reliable despite its faults. "If I'm buying a new computer, I'm going all out. I'll need something I can count on for a long time. I have a lot of books to write." Strangely, her heart soared at the very possibility.

"You'll be sending me a copy of this one you're writing now, right? Signed to the cowboy who inspired it?" Wade wore a goofy grin that made her laugh, but underneath that laugh was reality. A reality that said she couldn't even hand him a copy in person. She'd have to stick one in the mail to a town that'd soon be a distant memory, captured only in the pages of her book.

CHAPTER 14

 *ade*

"Are you happy with it?" Wade asked Trish as he slowed the truck for a fast food place. Trish had closed the store down, meticulous about getting the perfect laptop for a writer. "One with the right programs, lightweight, and of course, the perfect color." She'd ticked these off on her fingers as they walked the store's aisles. He almost felt bad that they didn't have a *sparkly* option. She'd have been over the moon, but the time it took did limit their dinner options.

"Yes!" She hugged the box to her chest. "I can't wait to get back and transfer all my files and start writing on my *new* laptop. Wade, I've never had a new one before! I even bought The Dinosaur used because it was all I could afford at the time."

"I know you'll get good use out of it." Her giddiness was contagious, putting Wade in a good mood as they ordered through the drive-thru and maneuvered back onto the road. "Can't eat in the truck. Grams was nice enough to let us borrow it, but she'd kill us if she thought we ate in here."

"I'm sorry I took so long to decide—"

"Don't be. It just means we get a tailgate meal with a view of the stars." Wade regretted the words as soon as they were out. They were much too romantic for his friends-only policy. The last thing he wanted to do was send mixed signals. She'd been through enough today without him adding complications.

"You're too good to me, Wade. I feel positively spoiled. And you're even giving me inspiration for another scene to write!"

Her eyes sparkled, making Wade wish he could do something—anything—to keep that sparkle alive forever. That Hank fellow had done a pretty good number on dulling it. Wade hoped to never meet him, because if he did, he'd have a hard time not punching the guy.

Wade turned onto a narrow road, away from the main drag they'd taken into town. He followed it until it turned to gravel and snaked around to the left.

"This is the part where you murder me, isn't it?"

Wade grinned at her then, raising his eyebrows until she laughed. "You've been living in the city too long." He pulled into an empty lot with a partial view of town. The nearest home was at least half a mile away, allowing the stars to light their way. He only knew about it because Allen had bragged about bringing a date here once.

"We can eat on the tailgate," he said. "Grab that blanket on the back seat."

Trish met him at the back of the truck and waited until he lowered the tailgate to spread the blanket. "It's so pretty out here. Even with the glow of the town, there are ten times as many stars out as there are from my little apartment balcony."

"Dinner is served," Wade said, setting the two bags of food next to Trish and effectively creating a barrier between them. "Better get some before it turns to ice. Won't take long out here."

Once their meals were divided up, Trish tilted her head back toward the sky. "I can see why you never left Starlight. If I'd grown up out here, I would have stayed, too."

Wade battled both reluctance to kill her light-headed mood and curiosity about all things that made Trish Meadows the woman she was today.

Curiosity won out. "You said you moved around a lot as a kid," he asked cautiously. "Why was that?"

After a deep sigh and a few fries, Trish answered. "I was dropped off as a baby at the back door of a fire station. My parents, whoever they are, didn't even bother to leave a note. I know nothing about who they are or why they gave me up. Only that I was three weeks old when they left me forever." Trish grabbed a few more fries, but before she took a bite added, "I'm only guessing that it was both of them because the security footage caught a blurry image of a man and a woman. But it was never enough to identify anyone."

Wade's heart felt as if it had cracked open at her admission. He only knew his parents until he was five, but he'd never once wondered if they loved him. "Trish, I'm . . . That's awful."

Trish shrugged. "I can't change it." But her easy words now wobbled. A tear glistened. "I've always wanted a family. One who took me in as their own. Instead, I was bounced around from foster home to foster home. Never figured out what I did to make none of them want to keep me."

He shoved the food and drinks back behind them and scooted next to Trish, drawing her into his arms as she broke down. She tucked her head beneath his chin and her tears soaked through his shirt. He couldn't imagine it, either. She had a big heart, and even bigger dreams. What parents wouldn't want to adopt her as their own? "My parents would have loved you."

The thought ripped inside him, because he knew it was true. In another lifetime—one where they were still alive—they would have adored Trish Meadows. He might've brought her for dinner at the ranch to meet them.

"And Grams, Kate, Allen, Chet, they talk about you all the time," he said because he had to keep talking or he'd break down, too. "You're the most exciting thing to come to the ranch in a long time."

"I'm a paying guest," Trish said, but there was a hint of laughter through the tears. "Of course they talk about me. And Chet hasn't said a thing about me. No way. I don't think he talks."

Wade chuckled at that, because it was true. Chet was a man of very few words. "I'll have you know that you've made Grams very happy by being here and torturing me," he said, flashing her a purpose-fully cheesy smile when she looked up. "She hasn't been this happy since . . . Well, you know we lost Grandpa last year. If she could, she'd keep you."

Trish pulled back from his embrace and wiped at her cheeks with the backs of her hands. "What was your grandpa like?" She reached behind them for her drink, but she didn't scoot away.

"A great man. Loved his family and loved his land." *Unlike his only surviving son.* Wade closed his eyes and took a deep breath. He didn't need to bring up Bill or that call tonight. Tomorrow, he'd talked to Grams about it. But tonight, he'd leave it alone. "The ranch was a way of life to Grandpa. A symbol of pride. He taught me how to ride a horse. How to rope a calf. How to drive a tractor. Even how to muck out a stall."

Wade found it easier to talk about him than it had been before, but it still stung to think he'd never see Grandpa in the kitchen again over a cup of daybreak coffee, as he used to call it.

"You miss him."

"Yeah. A lot." Wade found he needed to keep talking or risk falling apart. No point in both of them crying tonight. "I wonder how I'm doing, running the ranch. Wonder if he's up there." He nodded toward the stars. "Muttering under his breath each time I do something some lopsided way."

"I bet he's proud of you," Trish said. "I know your grandma is. Overheard her saying so to one of the other writers this morning. How you run things a lot like your grandpa. How you're so good with the animals the way he was."

He wanted to pull her close again, if only to make sure she didn't see him tearing up. Dang it, he didn't want to be all emotional tonight. "You done?"

"Yeah."

He finished off his burger and collected all the trash.

Spotting a trash barrel under the single light

pole on the opposite side of the vacant lot, he headed toward it. He needed a minute to compose himself. Things were getting too real with Trish. He had to step away or there'd be no hope at all for him.

If only he had never been ruined by grief's ugly face, maybe he could let himself fall without the fear of losing it all.

$$\sim$$

TRISH

TRISH WROTE LATE into the night, finally turning both the clock on her nightstand toward the wall and her phone screen face down when she grew tired of them mocking her. Though her one-on-one with the literary agent was tomorrow before lunch—now today—Trish couldn't bring herself to stop writing. The trip to Gillette had been inspiring.

Or maybe it had been Wade himself who was inspiring.

Trish pushed away her new feather-light laptop and stood to stretch her legs. Then she proceeded to pace around the bed. Shadow lifted a sleepy head, confused why they were even still awake. She'd followed Trish upstairs earlier, refusing to take no for an answer.

Friends. He'd told her it was best if they stayed friends.

Of course it made sense. Trish would head back to Omaha in three days. She might keep in touch with Kate over social media or Grams via Christmas cards. But she doubted she'd hear from Wade once she left. He didn't seem interested in Facebook or anything of the like. And half the time, he left his phone behind.

Yet, he'd held her in his arms and let her cry herself clean out of tears on the tailgate when she fell apart on him. His embrace brought her comfort. Made her feel safe. Protected. Henry only knew she didn't have any family. He'd never asked why. Trish had known Wade all of a few days, and he genuinely seemed to care about the answer.

Too restless to keep writing, Trish slipped downstairs hoping to swipe a cookie from the kitchen and sit outside in the crisp night. Maybe some fresh air would be the key to quieting her racing thoughts. Shadow crept along at her heel.

A few steps from the kitchen, Trish caught a flicker of light as if someone had opened and closed a door, but left it ajar. Her heart raced at the thought of it being Wade, as restless for sleep as she was.

Before Trish could make her escape, Shadow trotted away toward it.

"Shadow!" Trish whisper-called. "Come back! Shadow!" But she didn't seem interested in listening.

"I'll give you a treat," Trish tried, but her fluffy tail disappeared around the corner, forcing Trish to follow.

Before she could catch up, Shadow was at the door in question and wedged her nose in the crack. Trish held her breath, wondering how she'd explain this if Wade was standing on the other side, missing clothes.

"Hey, girl." The voice didn't belong to Wade, but Lina. "Where'd you come from?" Her tone was quiet, something about it despondent. Trish heard a sniffle.

"I'm sorry, Lina. She snuck off—"

"Trish? What're you doing awake at this hour?"

"Writing." It wasn't a lie, merely a partial truth. She walked to the doorway and stopped. Lina had a photo album open on her bed, a box of tissues nearby. "I'm sorry I let her wander off."

"Nonsense." Lina tried to smile, but it seemed strained. "Shadow does what she wants, don't you girl?" The shepherd sat at Lina's feet, body pressed against her legs, head in her lap.

"Is everything okay, Lina?" Trish knew with a single glance that it wasn't. She wished she knew how to make it better. Easier.

"Just reminiscing." She waved a dismissive hand. "If you're hungry, I can fix you something to eat." Another sniff accompanied her words.

Cookies all but forgotten, Trish bravely stepped

into the room and dropped onto the bed beside Lina, placing her hand on top of the woman's. "Pictures of your family? I'd love to see them." This could be a mistake, she knew. Maybe her request would make the poor woman burst into tears.

Lina squeezed her hand and let go to reach for the album. "They're from my wedding day. *Our* wedding day. This is my husband, Cecil. Wasn't he handsome?" For the next hour, Lina explained each picture on each page, and described the day in detail, all with love in her voice. Trish found herself completely drawn into the story, asking several questions.

"It was the most chaotic, wonderful day of my life." Lina's head turned and locked on an oak door. "Do you want to see my dress?"

"You still have it?" Tingles of excitement ran through Trish. She'd always wondered what it would be like to have a grandmother of her own, to hear these wonderful stories, and share special moments with.

"Of course." Lina disappeared into the closet for a moment and returned with a plastic see-through garment bag that showcased a beautiful satin gown with lace sleeves. Small crystals were woven into the lace that flowed across the neckline. "It isn't much, but—"

"Isn't much? It's beautiful!" Trish hopped to her feet to take a closer look. "Absolutely perfect." It saddened Trish to think it might never get worn again but stay in the garment bag for the rest of its days.

Lina hung it from a hook on the inside of the closet door, her hand reaching to the bag. "Cecil sure loved this dress."

"Has anyone else worn it?" Trish asked.

"I offered to let Kate wear it on her wedding day, but that girl already had her dress picked out. Strong-willed, that one is. Always marched to the beat of her own drum." Lina sighed as she lifted the dress off its hook and carried it back into the closet. "It's a shame. Too old-fashioned for kids nowadays I suppose."

Trish almost blurted, *"I'd wear it."* But the words tangled her tongue, and rightfully so. "Maybe the woman who marries Wade would want to wear it."

"Only if he gets past this whole notion that he'd rather be alone," Lina mumbled from inside the closet. With a click of a string light switch, the closet went dark and Lina closed the door behind her. "I suppose I should get to bed. And you need some sleep before your session with Taylor. You'll want to make a good impression."

A yawn ensued as she herded Shadow out of the bedroom. Trish stopped at the doorway, turning toward Lina. "Thank you. I've never had any grand-parents to share their stories with me."

"Of course, dear." Lina met her at the doorway and wrapped her in a heartfelt hug. "I'll see you in a few hours. Get some rest." With the door halfway closed, she added, "And Trish?"

"Yes?"

"Please don't mention me in this state to Wade. He worries too much about me."

"Your secret's safe with me."

rish

EVERY SINGLE FEAR she'd been repressing since she got in her car and drove to Wyoming came whooshing back. Trish wiped her sweating palms against her jeans, trying to ignore the way her chest kept thudding as she waited for Taylor to appear on the laptop screen. Lina had set up a Skype call with the literary agent an hour ago in a small office under the living room staircase. Taylor had already met with two authors, and was on a quick coffee break before she sat down with Trish.

What if her story stank? What if it was the worst thing Taylor had ever read? What if she told her to give up her dream of being a writer?

"Hello there." A woman, maybe a couple of years older than Trish, with dark hair pulled into a bun, appeared on the screen as a voice came through the computer's speakers. "You must be Trish. I'm Taylor."

"Yes, I'm Trish. H-hi." Could she sound any more nervous?

Taylor's reading glasses were visible on the top of her head as she stirred something just below the screen, only her spoon's handle visible. Trish tried relaxing, but the stiffness of her purple flower-patterned chair made it difficult. She tried to calm her breathing with slow controlled breaths, hoping Taylor wouldn't notice.

Taylor reached for the reading glasses and slid them on. "I've had a chance to look over your first three chapters." No small talk. No *How's your day?* Just right down to it. Which, when one considered she only had twenty minutes scheduled for the discussion, made sense. She shuffled some papers, which Trish assumed were *her* pages.

"Yes?" It was the only intelligible word that escaped her lips.

Taylor kept moving her glasses, putting them back on the top of her head. "The premise has promise. There's an adorable meet cute for your two main characters."

But? Because there was a huge *but* in those unspoken words.

"But I don't have a real *sense* of who these characters are or what they want most. I'm not invested in their story." Taylor sat back against the chair. "I'm not sure what your heroine's motivation is. What her main goal is."

"Oh."

"Frankly, I don't much care for your hero. He's flat. Uninteresting. Two-dimensional. I had higher hopes for him after the way they met at the dinner party with your heroine spilling a bowl of cocktail sauce on his suit. But I don't buy why your heroine is even *interested* in him."

"I see." Trish fought back the tears. She would *not* cry until she was alone in her room. No one would see her dreams shatter around her. This was exactly the kind of feedback that Henry would use as an I-told-you-so moment.

"Your heroine, she intrigues me," Taylor said. "Can't say she won me over. But she has hope. She did make me nearly spit out my coffee on the first page."

Trish perked a bit at that comment.

"But axe your hero." Taylor leaned forward. "Sorry hun, but you need to start over on him. He's . . . just not a likable character."

When one considered her hero had been loosely based on Henry, that sort of made sense. Henry was also flat and uninteresting outside of his job and golfing hobby. "You're right. He's completely boring."

"A real dud, I'm afraid."

Trish sputtered a burst of laughter and had to cover her mouth. Of course he was. "Sorry, it's just that that word's been tossed around a lot lately. You're absolutely right."

"Trish, your writing is strong. You have a great ability to pull the reader into the story with your prose, but if your characters aren't cutting it, readers don't keep turning the page. I'll email you my notes once I've met with everyone. It was great to meet you."

Uh-oh. She was being dismissed already. They'd been talking for hardly ten minutes. "Would you be interested in taking another look?" Trish asked, desperate to keep the agent on the line. "If I fixed it?"

Taylor stirred the contents of her mug again as her eyes dropped to something offscreen. "I think you should definitely keep writing, Trish. But I'm sorry. I just didn't fall in love with this story; I'll have to pass."

A wave of defeat knocked Trish right in the chest. "Thank you for your time, Taylor." She'd have to leave now, while most of her dignity was still intact. She was tired of crying in front of everyone.

"Trish?"

Halfway out of her seat, Trish stopped. "Yes?"

"You're talented. I'm just not convinced that *this* is your story."

"I-I started another one. One about a romance novelist and a brooding cowboy." It was a long shot, but at this point what did she have to lose? "I'm halfway through it, and it needs some polishing, but—"

"That sounds more interesting already."

"It does?"

"Sure." Taylor tapped her spoon against her mug. "Why don't you send me your first chapter of that one? And a synopsis when you're finished? I'd be willing to take a look. Can't make any promises, but I could at least give you some feedback."

"Thank you! That would be wonderful."

Trish slipped out of the office, feeling better than she expected considering how big a flop her first try had been. Didn't even seem salvageable from what Taylor said. But Trish thought she might be able to fix it. Take out the CEO and replace him with a good cowboy stuck in the city against his will? Sure, there just might be hope.

With several ideas already brewing, Trish made a beeline for the stairs. But two steps up, she was stopped.

"How did it go?" Glenda asked, hands clapped together at her chest. "Did she like your story?"

Trish dropped back down to the main level. "Nope."

"Oh, sweetie, I'm sorry."

"It's okay. I know what I have to do to fix it." Before Trish could tell her about the agent's interest in her next book, Glenda cut her off.

"You know, you don't *have* to go the traditional route. There are plenty of talented, successful writers who self-publish because of the creative freedom they get with that choice. Some even making a living at it. I know at least one anyway." Glenda winked at her. "It's a lot of work, but if you decide to try it on for size, let me know. I have a great editor I can recommend. And my cover artist is dynamite."

A smile formed. Trish had never considered publishing on her own. It was scary, unfamiliar territory. And she was sure Henry would never give her credit as an author if she went that route. No contracts and all that jazz. But now that she didn't give a hoot what Henry thought, the idea *had* attractive qualities. "I might come talk to you later, Glenda."

"I'd love that." Glenda glanced toward the top of the stairs. "Headed to write?"

"Yep."

"Let me know if you need to talk through any more plot hang-ups."

"Thanks, Glenda." And Trish meant it. Before this retreat, she hadn't met any other writers in person. Now she had a small tribe of them she could call friends.

She scurried up to the top of the stairs, Shadow close on her heel. But before she could slip into her room, Glenda called up, "You'll want to be ready for dinner at five. Lina wanted me to remind you. It's some special dinner with your cowboy, so dress up a bit."

"Dinner with—" But Glenda'd vanished into the office under the stairs for her turn with the agent. Trish pulled out her itinerary and checked what was on it for this evening. There was an author dinner in town at a restaurant called The Starlight Grill. But nothing about a personal dinner with a cowboy. Trish looked at Shadow. "There are certainly a lot of changes to this itinerary."

With the dinner plan adjustment a complete mystery to Trish, she opted for one of the outfits Mindy had packed—a short burnt orange dress with lace-up detail and bell sleeves, a pair of tights, and the cowgirl boots she couldn't seem to stop wearing. They were incredibly comfortable, and she loved how they made her feel.

At ten 'til five, Trish ventured downstairs to find a quiet house. A folded note card sat upright on the kitchen counter with her name. She looked around for signs of anyone, but the house was completely quiet except for the occasional settling creak. Perhaps everyone else was in town.

Dinner for you and Wade is in the oven keeping warm. Ready to serve. Dessert and a bottle of wine in the fridge. We'll be back by eight.

"Grams, I think we need to talk after dinner—" Wade's voice echoed throughout the empty kitchen as the bathroom door swung open. He was rubbing a towel over his wet hair, and his shirt was missing.

Trish swallowed.

"Hey, you seen Grams?"

Words failing her, she held up the card to him, trying hard and failing to keep her eyes off the muscle definition Wade's shirts had been hiding this whole time. For as many times as he held her against him, Trish suspected he was in shape, but to witness it in person was a whole other matter.

Wade read the card, his head shaking as he did. He plopped it back on the island. "Should've known." He seemed unaware that he was only wearing a pair of jeans and a towel over one shoulder. "If you don't want to do this dinner thing—"

"We should at least see what your grandma made," Trish cut in, desperate for something to occupy her so she'd stop staring at his chest. She skittered around the island to the oven. With a potholder, she lifted lids from two covered plates.

Wade leaned over the island. "Country fried steak. Of course."

"You make it sound like that's a bad thing."

"Grams makes the best country fried steak in the county. It also happens to be my favorite."

Trish pulled the plates out, set them on the stove-top, and closed the oven. "I'm a little lost on the problem."

"It's nothing."

"If it's me—"

"It's not you. Grams has been dodging me because, well, never mind. I guess we shouldn't let a perfectly good dinner go to waste." He slipped back into the bathroom and returned buttoning up a shirt. It wouldn't help Trish to concentrate better, covering up those strong muscles. They were burned into her memory.

"I'll bring the plates if you want to grab something to drink?" Trish practically ran out of the kitchen, embarrassment heating her cheeks. It was evident Wade expected a different dinner arrangement. The itinerary omission of this particular private dinner made a little more sense now.

"Wine or beer?" he called from the other room as Trish set the plates down across from each other.

"A beer would be great." Then she shuffled the plates next to each other. No, that didn't seem right either. Finally, she settled on one plate at the head of the table and one off to the side.

"You okay with a wheat beer? It's not fancy, but it's the lightest one in—" He froze a few steps from the table.

"What's wrong?" Trish looked around the table, certain she'd screwed up the arrangement of the place settings. *Too intimate?* She should have kept them across the table from each other.

"That's my grandpa's place." He nodded at the spot at the head of the table. "Haven't sat there since I was a kid looking to rile him up."

"You're the head of the ranch now, right?" Trish took a step toward him, reaching for the sweating bottles and setting them on the table by their settings. "I'm sure he'd be happy to have you sit in his place. I'll be right back. Forgot silverware."

At the rattle of the silverware drawer, Shadow made her first appearance since Trish dressed for dinner. With the length of her stretch, Trish assumed she'd just woken from a good, long nap. Trish could use one herself with how late she was up the night before. Maybe tonight, she'd go to bed early. But as she walked back toward the dining room table, her heart sank a little. Tomorrow was her last full day at the ranch. The day after, she'd have to get on the road.

"Wade, is everything okay?" Trish asked when she noticed his hands on the top of the chair, his head lowered. She touched his arm, but he kept his head bowed.

"Let's eat."

"Hey." She reached a gentle hand to his chin and turned his face toward her. Tears glistened in his eyes. Even through the shirt he'd put on, she could see the tension in his shoulders. "Talk to me."

"My uncle wants to sell part of the ranch. I think Grams might go for it."

"What?" She couldn't believe the words could be true. Lina loved the ranch as much as the rest of them. Trish saw that in her glowing eyes, in the way she talked about their ranch every day. "What makes you think that?"

Wade pulled out his chair and nodded for Trish to do the same. "Money's been tighter than I realized. Grams didn't let on how tight, though."

Act natural. Cutting into her country fried steak, Trish asked, "But aren't you the one running things? Wouldn't that include the books?"

"Grams has always been pretty secretive about her bookkeeping methods. I figured it was because my uncle Bill always got dollar signs in his eyes whenever money was brought up. Guess I should've known something was up when she still wouldn't share that with me after he left for Europe."

"Maybe that's why she put this retreat together?" Trish suggested. "Maybe if she did a few more . . ."

"I saw the books this morning. This retreat—" he waved his fork in the air "—won't make a dent in what we need. Leave it to Bill to want to sell the best part of the ranch to some stranger."

"What part?"

Wade took his time taking a bite and swallowing before he answered. "North pasture. All hundred acres of it."

"That must be just a small corner of the ranch, right?" Trish asked and waited for a nod. "Would a hundred acres be so bad if it helped catch things up?"

Wade's fiery glare sent shivers through Trish, and not the good kind. The kind that let her know she'd said something very, very wrong. "The north pasture has the best grazing land we have."

There was something he wasn't telling her. She braved on, hoping to learn what it was. "What else is out there?"

Wade wiped his mouth with a napkin, tossing it on his empty plate. He took a swig of his beer before he asked, "You really want to know?"

"Yes."

He pushed back from his chair and grabbed both their plates. "Grab a jacket."

CHAPTER 16

IF WADE HAD BEEN on his own, he would've raced across the ranch. But with Trish as his passenger and Shadow insistent on joining them, he had to take the drive in the ATV easier. At first the slow pace grated on him. But with the sun illuminating the tops of the trees, more yellow by the day, some of Wade's tension lifted.

Near the top of a rolling hill, his small cabin peeked out from behind a couple of mature trees and they rolled to a stop. "We have a couple of these cabins on the ranch in different pastures," he explained. "Kind of like base camps if someone needs to stick around to keep an eye on things." He thought it might be best to leave out the detail about Chet spending two weeks out here a few summers ago to keep the herd safe from a lurking wolf.

"You should tell your grandma to stick writers who don't like people out here."

"Haven't met one yet," he said with a quick smile, feeling relief that they were back to bantering. He knew it was childish of him to hold her innocent, rational question against her. She hadn't grown up on a ranch. She didn't understand how sacred every acre was to a ranching family. Uncle Bill should, but Wade wouldn't take that frustration out on Trish.

"Oh."

Wade had called someone to come out next week to take a look at the well. But unless he could keep Grams from making any rash decisions about selling this part of the ranch—or any of it for that matter—he should probably hold off. If she chose to sell, there was nothing he could do to change her mind. But that didn't mean he had to make things easier for a new owner on his dime.

"Grams figured this one might be a little too rustic for a romance writer," he added because he didn't want to talk about the possibility this cabin might not be his indefinitely. "And it's kind of under construction."

Wade stepped off the ATV, Shadow immediately leaping from the back. The shepherd went right to sniffing along the deck, looking for her buddy, Squirrel. "You can get out here by the river, too, but it's a bit of a hike up that hill." He stepped around the ATV and reached for her hand. It fit perfectly into his own, and he found himself reluctant to let go, so he didn't.

"The deck looks new," Trish said once they stepped closer.

"I've been doing a little work out here, off and on," he admitted.

Squirrel poked his head around the side of the cabin, curious about the unfamiliar voice. Sometimes Allen or Chet came out and gave Wade a hand with the heavier work, but Wade had never brought a woman here before. First sight of Shadow, however, and the cat went back to hiding.

"Can you get here by road?" she asked. "Like with a truck?"

"It's a pretty rough one." He nodded to the overgrown dirt path. "Better for the four-wheeler. But my truck can get within a quarter mile. Then I walk in." Just another reason it didn't make sense for Bill to try to sell off the north pasture. Of course, Uncle Bill hadn't been out here himself in a few years. Likely he only remembered the view.

Wade unlocked the cabin's door, suddenly aware that he'd left cabinet doors scattered all over to let the stain dry. "It's a little messy right now," he warned.

But Trish hadn't even turned toward the front door. She had her phone raised and was snapping pictures. "I bet the sunsets out here are amazing. This view!"

"Give it about thirty minutes and you can see for yourself."

She turned toward him, bumping into his shoulder. "I get it now."

It rattled him how natural this all felt, standing so close on the deck of his personal sanctuary. "Get what?"

"I get why selling even a single acre would be impossible." Electricity crackled between them. "There's something magical about this land."

Wade could imagine the two of them standing on this deck seasons from now, Trish with her back nestled against his chest, his cheek tucked against the top of her head, watching the sunset with his arms around her. The thought jolted him, and he stepped away. "Let me show you the cabin." He opened the door wider, to hold it for her. "As I said, it's a little messy."

He flipped the light on. Shadow zipped inside to investigate every event and smell she'd missed over the past few days. Squirrel hopped up onto the porch and peeked his head around the door before ultimately darting inside. The two ran circles around each other in greeting.

"*This* is a base camp cabin for cowboys?" Trish slowly wandered the room, her eyes studying the refinished hardwood floors. Wade had spent an entire week sanding them down before they were ready for the cherry stain. She trailed fingers along the black granite surface of the island.

"Well, it was a little more rustic before I started renovating," Wade admitted.

Trish spun around and pinned him with a look. "Are you planning to move out here?"

Because Wade hadn't admitted to anyone that he actually was, he started gathering cabinet doors and lining them on the counters. A basket beneath the sink held the hinges, and he dug that out along with a drill. Anything to keep himself averted from Trish's too inquisitive stare. "I like my quiet." It wasn't a lie. More of an omission.

"You are, aren't you?" Trish rounded the island until she was standing hardly a foot away from him. Wade's traitorous heart thudded loudly in his ears.

Squirrel saved him, hopping onto the counter and meowing. "We shouldn't stay out here too late," Wade said. "Grams'll worry if she shows back up and we're not around."

Trish folded her arms, refusing to move out of his way. "This cabin . . . it's great for a temporary getaway. I mean, I could easily spend entire week-ends out here writing."

He dared to meet her eyes and caught a sparkle in them. "You could?"

"Well, duh! Have you *seen* the view?" Squirrel turned and strutted toward Trish, winning a scratch under his chin. "But Wade, wouldn't you get lonely living out here full time?"

He didn't think so. Grams would have Bill and Tabby when they returned from Europe to help fill the house with noise. Well, until Aunt Tabby booked another speaking tour. But he could come down for dinner a couple of nights a week. And Kate and Ty would surely visit when Eli made it into the world. Who'd notice if Wade slipped off quietly to his cabin to live? "I like the . . . peacefulness."

"The ranch is quiet."

"Sometimes."

"I think this cabin is great for the occasional escape, but you'll break your grandma's heart, moving way out here all by yourself. The road within a quarter mile? Where she can't even *get* to you." So Trish had seen through that little flaw. One of the perks to a rough, overgrown road was a limited number of visitors. Especially uninvited ones.

"Look, it's a ways off. I see that. But I need to build an addition."

"Addition?"

"You don't expect me to put my master suite out here in the open, do you?"

Trish raised an eyebrow. "You don't have running water."

"But I will." Wade stepped back and pointed to the sink. "I just need to have the well inspected. Which was supposed to happen next week."

"Have you talked to Grams?" Trish asked.

Wade shook his head as he switched out the drill batteries and prepared to get to work on the cabinets' hinges. Allen would probably call him a fool for working on his cabin when he had a beautiful woman with him so close to sunset. But Wade needed to stay busy or he'd boil up with anger again at his uncle's plan. "She's been avoiding me."

A soft hand covered his, preventing him from lifting the drill. "Then get creative."

"You do know who you're talking about, right?"

"She's probably overwhelmed. She has a house full of writers, a grandchild who might show up at any time, and she's already asked you to entertain me all week. Maybe she doesn't want to burden you. If she's avoiding you, then find a way to be in her path."

The glow of the setting sun kissed Trish's cheek. Wade had to stop himself from caressing that spot, because he very much wanted to. But in hardly more than a day, she'd be gone forever. "I'll talk to her tonight." It had to be soon because he wasn't sure how much time Grams had before Bill expected an answer.

"Good."

Shadow popped around the island, her nose reaching up to the counter toward Squirrel. The cat studied the extended nose for a moment. Shadow took the opportunity to give Squirrel a good lick. Squirrel arched his back and batted Shadow's nose, then proceeded to strut away. Shadow shoved her way around them to get to the cat, pushing Trish flat against Wade's chest.

His breath hitched, the air suddenly hard to inhale. She fit so perfectly against him, as if she was meant to be there. When those sparkling hazel eyes looked up at him, he was completely lost. His hand reached out of its own accord. His thumb caressed her cheek, gently hooking her chin and tilting it toward him. He no more had the power to resist the temptation to kiss Trish than he had to stop the sun from setting.

An inch away he paused, seeking permission. Giving Trish a chance to slip out of his arms, to run away. But her eyes dropped to his lips, and he closed the gap with a featherlight brush against her lips. The world around him spun in fast, dizzying circles. The kiss deepened, and he could feel it clear through to his bones. Falling felt an awful lot like soaring over the highest mountain tops.

Shadow let out a booming bark, breaking the trance.

Wade let out a heavy sigh. "We have a visitor." Shadow only barked at cattle and to announce newcomers. He reluctantly released Trish from his embrace and strode toward the window. Headlights flickered off. Allen hopped off his ATV and practically sprinted toward the front door.

Wade beat him there and opened it.

"There you two are!" He huffed, as if he'd been running a long distance.

"Did you push your four-wheeler here or something?" Wade teased.

"We've been looking for you everywhere!" Allen motioned for them to follow. "We gotta go. Kate's in labor!"

rish

"Anyone been able to get hold of Ty?" Wade asked from the front seat, next to Allen, as Trish held on the seatback for dear life. Her seatbelt had done little to reassure her with how quickly Allen raced into town, down rutted gravel roads, whipping around bends and berms toward the little town of Starlight. Trish, unused to this, felt as if she were on her first rodeo.

"Left him a voicemail," Allen said when Wade asked again. "And I think Kate sent him about three hundred texts. He's supposed to be over the Atlantic Ocean right now. She's been determined to make this baby wait until he gets home."

"I thought he had another week."

"He did. But they let him go home with the advanced crew."

Allen had filled them in on most of it before they even cleared the ranch gates. How the group of writers had him and Chet out to dinner at The Starlight Grill. "Wanted some *privacy* for you two, I guess."

Wade pounded a fist on his door.

"Seems the continuous winces of pain Kate tried to dismiss made Grams finally put her foot down. Insist they go to the hospital." Trish cringed, and mentally hit herself for brushing things off while Kate was in town yesterday.

"Was anyone going to clue me in?" Wade asked through gritted teeth as Allen turned for the hospital. Trish could feel the tension crackling in the cab of the truck. "I'm only her *brother*."

"Well, you've been a little busy lately. Also seem to have a habit of leaving your phone at the house and *disappearing*."

Trish felt guilty now for prying about the possible sale of the north pasture. Had she let it slide, Wade would've been home to hear his phone. Or if she'd simply said no when he asked if she wanted to see it, Allen wouldn't have had to run all over the ranch looking for them.

But then Wade might never have kissed her that second time like he meant it.

Starlight Memorial Hospital was tucked on the outskirts of town. At only two stories, it was a much smaller hospital than Trish would find in Omaha, but it appeared to be a newer addition to the town. Some of the landscaping was still dirt where grass would likely someday grow.

Allen slammed on the breaks at the entrance. "You two go. Grams is upstairs in the waiting room. Chet's there with her, trying to keep her calm. I'm gonna park. Be right up."

Wade practically fell out of the truck at that bit of news, Trish following closely behind, still a little taken aback that they brought her along. None of the other writers had come. They'd all gone back to the ranch under Glenda's instruction.

They'd been waiting on the front porch to take Shadow when Wade and Trish pulled up in the ATV they'd taken to the cabin. With both ATVs parked, and Allen racing to his truck to fire it up, Marti practically helped shove Trish inside with Wade.

The elevator ride to the second floor was filled with unspoken words. But Trish couldn't have picked the right words if she'd been given a lifetime to edit them. She glanced at Wade on the other side of the elevator. His arms were folded and he kept shifting his weight from one foot to the other.

"Wade—"

The elevator dinged and the door opened. He

didn't give her an opportunity to do anything other than follow.

They stopped at the main desk there. Trish asked, "Where's the waiting room for the maternity ward?"

Chet practically knocked them both over when they turned into the waiting area. "Good, you're here!" He looked back to Lina, who was pacing one of the aisles of chairs. "She might wear that carpet to the subfloor. I'm gettin' coffee."

Trish stood there stunned. She'd heard fewer total words from Chet during her entire ranch stay than he offered now. The poor guy seemed completely out of his comfort zone. "We got it, Chet." Wade clapped him on the shoulder and sent him on his way to the cafeteria. "Allen's on his way up, too. Go find something to drink."

"Grams." Wade went right up to her and placed two firm hands on her shoulders to stop the pacing. "What are you doing out here?"

"Didn't want Kate to see me fretting. It won't do her any good. Told her I needed some coffee. Her best friend is the nurse in with her now."

Whatever Wade said to Lina next, his voice was too low to hear. But it did convince her to ease into a chair. Wade sat in the one next to her and held her hands.

"I just hope Ty makes it in time," Lina said to Wade. "He should be here for the birth of his child!"

"He's coming as fast as he can."

Trish felt intrusive, hovering at the edge of the row of chairs while Wade and Lina talked only to each other. They should have left her behind at the ranch with the rest of the writers. *I don't belong here.*

Slipping out of the waiting room, Trish decided to track down some coffee. Chet might eventually bring some back, but he'd had that flight look in his eyes when they arrived. The least Trish could do was keep everyone supplied with fresh coffee while they waited out the arrival of the newest Holbrook.

Again she asked at the desk, then followed signs for the cafeteria through twisting hallways and an elevator ride down. She found herself wishing she had her phone; Mindy would know what to do.

Their first kiss had been impulsive, one that could easily be blamed on being caught up in the moment under the stars. It was a romance writers' retreat, after all, and Lina had gone to excessive lengths to make sure the atmosphere was inspirational.

But that second kiss . . . Her head was still spinning, her lips still tingling. Emotions ran rampant. It wasn't an impulsive kiss. It was a deliberate kiss.

Spotting Chet in the back corner of the cafeteria, phone to his ear, Trish found her way to the massive coffee maker. For the first time, coffee had no appeal to her. Her stomach twisted in anxious knots. What had that second kiss *meant?* The morning after tomorrow, Trish would get in her little car still covered with muddy handprints and drive away.

"Grams likes it with two sugars, no creamer."

"Hey, Chet." Trish poured two packets into one of the two black coffees and stirred it with a straw. No one had to tell her how Wade took his coffee. Nice and boring. "You get hold of Ty?"

Chet stared at her blankly for a moment. "Was talking to someone else." He helped himself to a Styrofoam cup and filled it with cappuccino at the machine beside the coffee.

"Wouldn't have pegged you for a cappuccino drinker."

"Guilty pleasure," he said with a shrug. Trish hadn't been able to get a good read on Chet since the first night he made an appearance at the fire pit. He appeared to be a couple of years younger than Wade. Quiet, kept to himself. But he seemed even more adverse to noise and commotion than Wade. And that was saying a lot.

"You in here hiding, too?" she asked. Anything to lighten things up.

"Not much I can do." He looked at the ceiling, as if they could see through the floor to the maternity ward. "How'd you end up here and the other writers got left behind?"

It was a fair question. One Trish had been searching for the answer for since she hopped in the truck with Wade and Allen. "Not sure, honestly." Her voice crackled slightly at the admission.

"*Hmm*."

With that undecipherable response, Trish felt the need to explain herself further. "I was with Wade. Out at that cabin? I think I got invited along by default." Perhaps it'd been quicker to bring her along than explain to her why they shouldn't.

Chet capped his cup with a lid. "You best be careful around Wade. He's left more than one broken heart in his wake."

Trish swallowed, unsure what to say to the ominous warning. Especially in this setting. No one had mentioned old girlfriends. Even though she'd brought up Henry multiple times, Wade had never done more than let her believe Kate was his wife. "He, uh, gets around?" she asked, afraid of the answer.

"He's a solid guy. Just likes being on his own." Chet nodded at her before he walked away with his guilty pleasure, leaving Trish frozen and unsure what to do with that bit of information.

WADE

THE TIMING WAS ALL WRONG. Wade couldn't bring

up Bill's call now, as much as he wanted to. With any luck, Kate's whole early labor thing would distract Grams and make her miss whatever short deadline she had to give him her decision. The books hadn't looked great, but they hadn't looked hopeless either. There were things they could do to make ends meet.

"Everything all right there?" Grams patted the hand he'd draped over the arm of the waiting room chair. "You seem a little distracted."

"Fine."

"It's Trish, isn't it?" A mischievous twinkle lit up her eyes.

"What? Grams . . . no." Wade had to put an end to whatever matchmaking fantasy his grandma had cooked up. It didn't matter that Trish made him smile when he wanted to be sour, or that she seemed to take to animals almost as well as he did, or even that the anticipation of another kiss made his pulse erratic.

He'd gotten too close to the edge of a cliff. Allen's interruption had saved him from taking a plunge he couldn't return from. Two more sunrises and she'd be gone for good, and it would get easier to forget she'd ever tempted him to lose himself completely. "Look, she's a nice lady. But Grams, you have to stop this whole setup thing."

"I don't know what you're talking about." Grams put a hand on her chest. "You were merely her chaperone this week. The cowboy inspiration for her next novel. I just helped bring that inspiration to life for her . . . through *you*."

Wade let out a little laugh. Soon, they were both laughing so hard tears came to their eyes. "So, you admit it!"

"I didn't draw those crayon hearts, though!" Lina teased.

"Yeah, found out that was Allen."

"Look Wade, you can't be afraid to open your heart. Yes, it hurts to someday have to let them go. But I wouldn't change the time I had with your grandfather for anything. If I had been too afraid of losing him, you wouldn't even be here right now."

Wade squirmed uneasily in his seat. He wasn't ready to have a conversation like this. "She goes home Sunday. Nothing changes that." It didn't matter how many times someone told him it was okay to let himself fall for someone, fall completely. For him, no reward outweighed the risk. Not after all the grief he'd witnessed in his lifetime. Grief caused by loving someone too much. If he was consumed with grief, who would run the ranch? Certainly not his greedy uncle.

Grams patted his hand again. "You could change that."

It was time to change the subject, and Wade knew what would do that quicker and more successfully than anything. "I heard Bill wants to sell off the north pasture."

The demeanor in Grams' face changed immediately from light and heartfelt to cold and rigid. "Eavesdropping on my phone conversations, Wade?"

"Not intentionally, no." But when the stern expression didn't soften, Wade knew he had to come clean. "Bill called that day before the photoshoot. Told me all about his plan. I . . . may have forgotten to mention it."

"Wade James Holbrook!" Lina clapped her hands against her legs. "This isn't your decision to make. Or your information to keep from me."

With a quick glance around the waiting area, hoping they hadn't invited unwanted attention, Wade lowered his voice in reply. "Grams, I saw the books. You left them out." His words started to tremble the more he spoke, so he stopped, hoping desperately that Grams would tell him he was wrong. That he saw something unfinished or miscalculated. "Things don't look good."

"Well, that's because they aren't."

Wade's stomach tangled at the confirmation of what he'd feared most. Here he'd been sinking all his extra cash into a cabin, toying with the idea of an addition, when all along he should have been using that money to help Grams. No point in fixing up a cabin on a piece of land they couldn't afford to keep. "So, you're going to sell it, then?"

"I haven't made up my mind," Grams said. "I have two more days."

Wade felt an ounce of hope in that admission. Two days might just be enough to figure out an alternative.

"It's a good offer. Double what I'd ever get for it otherwise. And if I don't take it," Grams added, "Bill says the offer's off the table for good."

CHAPTER 18

THE NIGHT WORE ON. Trish tried her best to keep Wade, Lina, and Allen supplied with coffee. Chet refused to have more than one cup of his cappuccino, then he switched to water. But by midnight, Trish could hardly keep her eyes open.

She wanted to head back to the ranch and curl up with a loveable German shepherd in her bed, but she wasn't about to ask anyone to drive her. The entire family was on pins and needles waiting for someone to tell them it was time, each one taking a turn to sit with Kate.

If only she had her new laptop, at least she could

get some writing in. Instead, she dozed off and on, stirring awake sometime around four.

"You holding up okay?" Wade stood in front of her chair, extending a cup of coffee.

She pushed herself into a sitting position, terrified that she looked a wreck. The too-much makeup she'd applied for their date the night before was surely smudged around her eyes. With a few pats of her hands, it was evident that the hairspray had formed sharp, odd angles in her short hair. "Is it black?" she asked, though right now she didn't really care. She'd drink anything that would bring a little bit of warmth to her bones.

"I fancied it up, just for you."

The sentiment, and Wade's flashed smile, warmed her. Gave her a tiny ping of hope that maybe there was a future with this cowboy. "Thank you."

He dropped into the seat next to hers and sipped on his own cup.

She looked around the waiting room, but Wade was the only one she recognized. "Where is everyone?"

"Grams is in with Kate. Allen went to get Ty from the airport. They managed to get him on a puddle jumper to Gillette. Should be back anytime. Chet's been good at hiding."

In other words, they were finally alone with nothing to do but wait. Now had to be as good a time as any to talk. But the words wouldn't form. Instead, Trish dared to rest her head on his shoulder. She felt him tense. Worried she'd overstepped some invisible line, she pulled away. Chet's words echoed in her mind. Maybe public displays of affection were off limits.

Trish readjusted herself and sat up, cupping both hands around her coffee. With a deep breath, she braved on. "When I first came here," she started. "Why did you think it was better for me to believe that you were married?"

Wade didn't answer at first. Just let out a deep sigh. "Trish, I'm exhausted. This really isn't the best time to talk."

Her first instinct was to apologize, because of course it wasn't. But Trish had spent half her relationship with Henry apologizing for things that didn't warrant an apology. She was done being that girl. "No, it's not the best time," Trish said. "But time isn't something we have a whole lot of left."

"Exactly." Wade ran both hands over his face. "You're leaving, Trish. Nothing changes that." Was Wade dismissing what was happening between them?

"You knew that from day one. So why'd you kiss me?"

"I don't . . . It was a mistake."

Trish shot up out of her chair, her heart pounding infuriatingly in her chest. "You're lying."

A few heads turned at her accusation, but she didn't pay them any mind. He'd taken his time with that kiss, drew her into it until the rest of the world faded around them. He'd even given her a chance to pull away. "It was very intentional. I was *there*, remember?"

Wade reached for her hand and pulled her back down to her chair. Jolts of electricity skittered up her arms at the contact, and from the widening of his eyes, she knew he felt it, too. How could he possibly deny that there was something between them? Something stronger, more vibrant than either could comprehend? Something *real*.

"I can't give you what you need, Trish." When she met his deep blue eyes, she saw pain in them. "I'll never—"

"We're here!" Allen bellowed as he ran into the waiting room, a tall man dressed in a military uniform right on his tail. "Is he here yet?" Allen's attention was directed at Wade, waiting for the shake of his head.

Wade extended her an apologetic look before he abandoned his seat to welcome his brother-in-law home from war. She watched the hearty hugs from her seat, feeling more out of place by the minute. Wade led the expectant father toward Kate's room.

"You're still here?" Allen took a seat in the row behind her in the corner, letting out a big yawn as he did.

"It's a long walk back to the ranch."

Allen chuckled at that, and she felt more at ease than she'd been since arriving at the hospital. Allen had an easy way with people that made them feel welcome, much like Lina. "You still planning to head back to Omaha?"

"You make it sound like I have another choice." Because the reality was, she didn't. She had an apartment. Bills to pay. A cubicle job that was expecting her in her seat first thing Monday morning. Maybe Wade had a point. It was a romantic, whimsical idea to think she could abandon her life in such an impulsive way, and for what? A possible relationship with a cowboy she met only a few days ago? What if it didn't work out? She'd be stuck all alone in Starlight, Wyoming while her best and only friend was hundreds of miles away.

"You going back to that stiff corporate guy?" Allen tipped his hat forward over his eyes and folded his arms after another yawn.

That question was easier to answer. "No. That chapter of my life's over." Henry had texted her a couple more times, each a little closer to an apology than the last. But Trish hadn't bothered to respond. Maybe he'd get the hint that she'd moved on. "Allen, do you think—" But soft snores came from behind her, leaving her alone with her thoughts.

Trish wished her life were a romance novel. Maybe then, the writer in her could figure out how long it would take Wade to come around, or what words she could use to help him open his heart to her. At least then she'd have a guarantee that they'd have a happily ever after. But the reality was, she wasn't so sure this story—with Wade—*had* a happy ending.

It was a couple more hours before there was any news on Kate and the baby. Wade had been in and out of the waiting room, but now he was careful to avoid Trish. Time was dwindling, and so was her hope.

She had never felt about anyone the way she felt about Wade. She'd never felt such a spark and sense of belonging with one man before. Certainly not about Henry. Her toes had never curled at any of Henry's kisses, that was for certain.

She might even be in love with him.

But how could they make it work?

"Eli is here!" Lina announced, her hands clapped together against her chest. Pure joy twinkled in her eyes. "I'm a great-grandma!"

Trish hopped out of her chair to give the woman a big hug and was squeezed breathless as a result. "Congratulations, Lina! I'm so happy for you and your family." Trish meant the words, meant them so much tears brimmed her eyes.

"I can't wait for you all to meet him. Allen, you'll have to— Allen!"

Lina navigated to the row behind Trish and shook Allen awake. Wade took what Trish could only describe as reluctant steps to join them in their little corner of the waiting room. "They're getting everything situated now. It'll be a couple of hours before Kate is all moved and settled in her new room."

Wade smiled, trying to hide the exhaustion in his droopy eyes. *Has he slept at all?* Trish had to tamp down the urge to go to him and offer her shoulder for her him to lean against. He looked as if he might drop at any moment. But the memory of how quickly he'd tensed at her touch kept her frozen in place.

"Why don't we grab some breakfast at Mabel's?" Allen suggested. "I, for one, would prefer to meet my second cousin on a full stomach."

"Why don't the rest of you go?" Lina suggested. "I'll wait here in case—"

"Grams, you need to eat," Allen insisted, turning her shoulders to steer her toward the door. "You most definitely are going."

"But—"

"I can stay," Wade offered.

"You need to eat, too," Lina scolded.

While the three of them argued about who should go, who should stay, and who should go find Chet, Trish tried to cut in a couple of times before she was successful. "You go. I'll stay. Lina, I can call you if anything comes up."

Lina placed a gentle hand on Trish's arm, the apologetic look in her eyes setting off alarms. "Hun, they won't tell you anything. You're . . ."

"Oh. Right. I'm not family." Trish nodded in hopes it would take the attention away from her eyes that were already filling with tears. She hadn't realized how badly she wanted a family until it become painfully clear she wasn't part of this one. An uncomfortable silence hovered until Wade chimed in.

"Look, Grams. You and Allen go grab a table at Mabel's. I'll round up Chet, and the three of us will meet you there. I'll let Ty know to call if they need us, okay?"

Lina gave in to that idea and let Allen usher her to the elevators.

They found Chet in the cafeteria, on his phone again. Instead of pacing this time, he'd commandeered a table to guarantee his privacy with a morning crowd filtering in for breakfast. He waved at them to let them know he was wrapping up his conversation.

"Who do you suppose he keeps talking to?" Trish asked Wade.

Wade shrugged his muscular shoulders, and memories of him without his shirt last night returned. "Your guess is as good as mine." They shared a brief, bashful smile. One that offered hope for a future.

"What's up?" Chet asked.

Wade filled him in on the latest developments, but he made a change to the breakfast plans. "You take Trish to Mabel's. Bring me back one of those bacon breakfast burritos. I'll call if anything comes up."

"You don't have your phone." Trish narrowed her eyes at him.

"I'll use Kate's."

Unlike the others, Chet didn't argue with Wade's insistence to stay behind. Trish felt him falling farther and farther away from her as they walked out into the lobby. Wade headed toward the elevator while Chet went for the exit.

Trish couldn't go now. Not with how they were leaving things. She had to try to get through to him or she might miss her chance. She left Chet at the main entrance as she hurried to the elevator. The door dinged, and Wade stepped in. Trish threw her hand against the door to keep it open.

"Wade, we need to talk."

"You need to catch up to Chet." He only briefly met her eyes before dropping his own to the floor. "He'll leave you behind when he's hungry."

"Wade—"

"You should go back to Omaha." His voice was low but firm. "There's nothing here for you."

His words sliced through her heart. The building suddenly felt confining. The walls and people scattered about suffocated her. She stumbled back and the elevator door closed, taking Wade up and away from her.

Her entire body trembled as she made her way outside.

Chet had his back leaned against a pillar, feet crossed at the ankles. "Ready?"

How could she possibly face Lina after what her grandson had just done to her heart? She yearned to curl up in bed the rest of the day and shut out the world. After such a final declaration, she was certain Wade would do his best to avoid her until she left. "Chet, is it too much a bother to drop me back at the ranch?"

CHAPTER 19

$\mathcal{W}$ade

THE MEMORY of Trish's beautiful hazel eyes watering and laced with pain would haunt him for the rest of his days. He never meant to cause her pain, but by opening himself to the possibility of falling, he'd hurt them both. Wade couldn't let her cling to some impossible hope that they could have a future. He couldn't give her the love she deserved.

The elevator opened, but Wade couldn't bring himself to go immediately back to the waiting room. Grams would be upset with him when he didn't join them for breakfast, but she'd soon be busy enough helping Kate and Ty with his nephew that she'd forget. Instead, he happened upon a sign with directions to a skywalk and headed that way.

Gloomy gray clouds blanketed the sky, threatening rain. It would mean waiting a few more days to bale hay. That yearly event always promised a very long couple of days, but the celebration after was always a blast. Except, Wade didn't feel a whole lot like celebrating. He felt more like running away to his cabin and living in solitude.

But his cabin might be sold to some unappreciative tourist with too much money in his pockets for his own good. There was no telling what kind of development that buyer would do to the land. Land that deserved to stay the way it was. But unless Wade could come up with another way to bring in several thousand dollars more, and soon, Grams might not have another option.

Why hadn't she been honest with him about the state of things? He was running the ranch now. He had a right to know what financial shape they were in.

After pacing back and forth along the skywalk a few times, he stopped in the center and looked out the north set of windows. That view showcased the Bighorn mountains in the distance, their snowcaps already more prominent than they'd been a week ago. Wade could imagine Trish snapping pictures with her cell phone, a glow in her expression.

"Hey, man." With his long legs, it only took Ty a

few strides to stand beside Wade. "Everyone else getting something to eat?"

"Yeah." Wade shoved his hands into the pockets of his Wranglers.

"They're getting Kate all moved. She kicked me out for a few minutes."

They both chuckled at that.

"Congratulations, Ty." He shook Ty's hand, feeling a bit like a jerk for not leading with that. "Can't wait to meet my nephew."

With radiance in his entire demeanor, Ty told him all about his newborn son. "He's already tall, just like me!" Ty should be exhausted, ready to drop, but he seemed to be riding a wave of happiness at the growth of his family. "Think you could help me get that nursey finished? I got it painted before I left, but Kate reminded me a few times that it's not done."

"Of course." It would be a good excuse to keep his distance from Trish until she left. It might make him a coward, but he couldn't bear to tell her good-bye. Not after the way he dismissed her in the elevator. "I can swing over later today."

Ty dug a buzzing phone out of his uniform sleeve pocket. "She's all moved. Want to meet your nephew?"

TRISH

TRISH TRIED and failed to sleep. Her heart ached in ways she hadn't even known were possible. Shadow licked her tear-soaked cheek, and Trish hugged her tight. Her apartment wasn't dog friendly, but maybe she could find a little house to rent that would allow one. If she could, she'd just steal Shadow. "You want to move to Omaha?" she asked the dog whose nose was inches from her own. Shadow's ears perked.

Since she'd skipped breakfast, Trish found herself famished. She'd thought about sneaking downstairs to scope out the kitchen for goodies, but she was too afraid she'd encounter one of the other writers. She couldn't face them, not after the agent had turned down her book *and* Wade had dismissed her as though she were no one special. Tomorrow, before she left, she'd find a way to paste on a smile and ask them how their sessions with the literary agent went. She hoped well.

Her phone buzzed on the nightstand. She contemplated turning it off, but her eyes caught the caller name—Henry—and she nearly came unglued with aggravation. She tried to ignore the call, but she had endured enough.

"What?" she barked.

"Whoa, babe, is that any way to greet the man in your life?"

Trish cackled. With the curious tilt of Shadow's

head, she figured it probably came out sounding a little bit like a Halloween witch's evil laugh. "You are so *not* the man in my life."

"Of course I—"

"Listen here, Henry." Trish had never been so bold with him before, but the coming tirade made her feel confident. Surer of herself than she'd ever been. Bravely, she stated, "You don't support my dreams to be a published romance author."

"Well, that's because—"

"I'm not done," she snapped. "I'm not going to waste away in a cubicle at some corporate job simply because it sounds more respectable to your friends and family. I'm done pretending to be someone I'm not. And I'm done with us. Have a nice life."

"But—"

"Good-bye, Henry." Trish ended the call, then proceeded to block his number. She had nothing more to say to him.

She dropped back against her pillow with a heavy sigh. Shadow combat-crawled up the bed until her head was close enough that she licked Trish on the cheek and rested her head on her chest.

Rain pattered against the roof, a sound that used to soothe Trish to sleep. But after more than ten attempts to close her eyes still failed, she pushed away the covers. She showered, tired of laying around and strangely renewed with energy. The refreshing shower was all she needed. She decided it was time to pack her things and lug her suitcase to her car.

"You're leaving without saying good-bye?"

Glenda stood on the porch, safely tucked under the roof out of the downpour, with folded arms and an unimpressed scowl.

Trish stepped onto the porch, trembling with the emotions she had been trying desperately to hold in. "Of course not." But tears leaked from her eyes. Glenda wrapped her in a soothing hug, despite her soaked clothes. "Everything's fine," Trish said immediately, afraid her tears might be misunderstood. "With Kate's baby. Healthy eight-pound baby boy, and his dad made it home."

"Lina called us an hour ago." Glenda rubbed a comforting hand along Trish's back.

"I-I just can't stay." The thought of seeing Wade again made her sure her heart would split open. The cold expression on his face as the elevator door closed would stick with her for a long time. Maybe forever.

"You're not driving all the way back to Omaha on no sleep, are you?" Glenda scolded. "Because I *will* wrestle those keys from you if I need to. Which gives me a great idea for my next book!"

They laughed together, and Trish pushed away the tears from her cheeks. "I'm going to stop in Rapid City. Stay the night at a hotel."

"No, you're not."

"What?"

"Give me half an hour. I'll have you follow me to my place. I live there, remember?"

"I don't want to be any trouble—"

"It's no trouble, dear. It would be a delight to have you as a guest. I'd feel better about you driving in this downpour if I kept an eye on you. Plus, I still owe you that conversation about my publishing team. We can talk books all day. No mention of cowboys at all. I swear." She gave her famous wink. "Unless you want to talk about how to put all this into a future book."

Trish wasn't sure how Glenda knew about Wade, but she didn't ask. "That sounds perfect."

"You wait here," Glenda instructed. "I'll be packed and ready to go in a jiff." She headed toward the stairs, but only made it a couple of steps before she spun around. "On second thought, hand me your keys."

"What?"

"Sweetie, you're emotional. I'm not going to risk you acting on some irrational impulse and driving away before I'm ready." Glenda reached out her hand. "I care about you. Hand 'em over."

Trish did it without much fight, touched by her new friend's concern. "I'll wait right here." She watched Glenda speed walk down the gravel road toward her personal cabin, a cardigan raised above her head to ward off some of the rain, until she disappeared around a bend toward the writer cabins.

Then her eyes fell on the driveway. In every romance novel she'd ever read, this was the moment when the hero came barreling down the drive to stop the heroine from leaving. He told her he was wrong; that if she left, his life would be empty and meaningless.

Only, Wade didn't come.

Trish left a heartfelt thank-you note for Lina on the kitchen island, a tear splashing onto the card and smearing the wet ink. But she didn't have time to write a new one.

Once Glenda's car was loaded and she'd given Trish back her keys, she wrapped Shadow in a hug. They both said quick good-byes to the other writers making them promise to keep in touch, and prepared to drive away from the Holbrook Ranch for good.

ade

"WHERE IS SHE?" Grams marched into the waiting room, right up to Wade, her pointed finger aimed at his nose.

"What are you talking about?"

"Trish. She didn't show up to breakfast." Her hands moved to her hips. "And neither did *you.*"

"Did you ask Chet?" But the words, strong in his head, came out of his mouth quiet and weak. The fire in Grams' eyes was enough to unsettle even the toughest man. "He was supposed to bring her to Mabel's."

Grams shoved a set of keys against Wade's chest. "Go get her."

"What?"

"I love you, Wade, I swear I do. But sometimes you're the densest of them all." Grams shackled his shoulders with a surprisingly painful grip and ratcheted him to his feet. "If you don't hurry, you're going to miss her."

"She's back at the house, Grams." He'd planned to avoid her as much as possible until she drove away tomorrow morning. But that was still almost a day away. He couldn't comprehend the urgency in Grams' voice.

"You really think she's waiting until tomorrow to leave?"

"What? How do you—"

"Because it's the same thing I did to your grandfather."

That caught his attention and left him speechless.

"Where do you think you get your stubbornness from?"

"But I should wait here, in case—"

"Eli was born a completely healthy baby. Kate is fine and recovering. Ty made it home safely. There's nothing for you to do here."

Because Wade was desperate to stay, he threw out his last best card. "But we need to figure out how to save the ranch. I can't stand the thought of you selling the north pasture. You have to give Bill an answer tomorrow, and—"

"And my answer to him is no." Grams took a deep breath, one that warned him he was trying her patience. "I'm holding more retreats."

"But that won't bring in enough money, Grams."

"We went through over a hundred applications to find Trish."

"What?"

"Oh, don't act so surprised. I wasn't about to let you live out the rest of your life bitter and alone without at least seeing what was out there. Plus, now I have a waitlist big enough to *fill* the north pasture." Grams shoved him toward the elevator. "You're clean out of excuses to stall."

"But—"

"Do you love her?"

"I just met her!" But Grams' question threw him for the biggest loop yet. Because he knew with every fiber of his being that he *was* completely in love with Trish Meadows. It twisted him up inside.

"You are. Admit it and go after her before it's too late."

"She deserves better. She deserves someone who can love her with his whole heart."

"Why can't that be you?" Grams pinned him with that question, her arms folded across her chest. "It's a *choice* Wade. Not some curse or disability."

"I'm scared, Grams." His words were barely more than a whisper.

"Love does that to a person," she said. "It's scary.

Risky. Terrifying. But it's also the most rewarding thing life has to offer. It's wonderful and *rare*. And if you don't hurry, you're going to miss her!"

Wade practically tripped over his own feet as he ran to the parking lot.

～

TRISH

TRISH MEADOWS WAS STUCK in the mud.

"This is seriously not happening!" Trish pounded her fists against her steering wheel, but it did little to change the fact she was stuck in the same stupid mud puddle that had welcomed her to the ranch almost a week ago.

She rolled down her window as Glenda pulled her car off to the side, hazard lights flashing, and rushed over. "Stuck?"

"Very."

Glenda extended a sympathetic look. "Sweetie, I think we're gonna have to wait for help. My little car can't pull yours out."

Trish groaned. "I'll call a tow truck." That was definitely better than running into a single Holbrook. If she did, she might just shatter into a million pieces.

"You have any cell service out here?"

"I always have service out here." She dug her

phone out of her purse after insisting that Glenda go back and park at the ranch until Trish could be rescued. She scrolled through her phone to find the number to her insurance company. With her road-side assistance option, they'd send a tow to her anywhere.

But her call dropped half a second after it dialed.

"No bars?" Trish whined. "But I always have bars."

She tried to flag down Glenda, but she'd already turned her car around and disappeared out of sight around the bend.

Trish opened her door a crack and peered down. Heavy raindrops pelted the deep puddle. Last time, it hadn't been raining yet she still managed to get covered in mud. Now that it was pouring down, Trish felt the odds stacked against her.

If she waited in her car for Glenda to figure out she didn't have cell service, there was no way she'd miss the entire Holbrook clan when they returned. But if she hiked back, the house had a landline. She could offer a towing company double if they'd hurry. No price was too high to avoid another encounter with the man who'd broken her heart. It might take weeks or months away from Starlight, but eventually she'd forget about Wade Holbrook. *Right?*

Trish stretched one leg as far as it would go, but even the very tip of her toe was destined to land in murky brown water. "I really need to take up yoga," she mumbled.

Her boots were packed out of spite, of course, in her trunk, and she was left with the same flip-flops she'd been wearing the day she arrived.

"The irony isn't lost on me," she said to the sky. But that only resulted in heavy raindrops splashing her in the eyes.

Tossing her shoes onto the passenger side floor, she winced as she dropped a toe down until it touched solid ground. Well, it *was* more soggy than solid. The rain soaked through her jeans, the denim making that awful sucking sound when she shifted to get a better balance in the puddle. Once her foot was flat against the ground, she whispered, "One down, Trish, one to go."

She then turned and reached for the car door, trying to ignore the squishy sensation of mud creeping between her toes, but her hands wouldn't quite touch. Another small, cautious step toward the door until she could touch it and swing it shut.

"Success!"

Trish was about to celebrate her victory when the roaring of a diesel engine startled her. She let out a little scream, reaching for a door she'd already closed.

But no, she lost her balance and slipped into the mud puddle. "Are you kidding me?" she screamed toward the sky.

"Where're your boots?"

Trish swallowed at the deep sound of Wade's voice cutting through the heavy rainfall. Why couldn't it be Lina or Chet? Chet would've hardly used ten words before he had her pulled out of the mud and on her way. "I packed them."

"If you ever hope to live on a ranch, you need to get used to wearing boots. They're made to get wet and muddy so you don't have to."

"Thank you, Mr. Obvious." Trish considered ignoring the hand he extended, but images of flailing around in the mud like a floppy fish scared her into accepting help. "And what do you mean if I hope to live on a ranch? I live in an apartment, remember? One *you* told me to go back to."

"But would you want to live on a ranch? Maybe one in Wyoming?"

Of course she wanted that, since the day she arrived. But it wasn't her life. Why was he torturing her with a fantasy? "That doesn't matter anymore."

Tears stung her eyes, but hopefully he wouldn't notice with the heavy rain. Her heart ached at the very sight of him. The blue of his eyes was a deeper color against the gray backdrop of the sky.

"I lied," he shouted over the sound of splashing rain.

"About boots?"

"About that kiss."

Trish's tongue caught in her throat. As she tossed

and turned in her bed for hours this morning, she'd fantasized about this very admission. But now that it was happening, her guard was up high. "I don't believe you."

He took her hands in his and pulled her against his chest. "I've been afraid." The brim of his hat gave them both a small reprieve from the rain. "Ever since my parents died, I've been scared of loving someone so much that losing them forever might actually kill me."

"No one falls in love with any guarantees, Wade."

"I know that now."

"What are you saying?"

"I love you, Trish."

"Y-you do?"

"No matter how much I want to fight it or run away, I'm at a complete loss. I've always been afraid of losing the person I loved and not being able to go on. And the thought of you driving away and never coming back is more than I can bear. It's worse to lose you that way, knowing I never fought for us to have a chance together."

"Do you really mean it? This isn't something Grams put you up to?"

"Well, she may have shoved me out the door. But the words, they're very much mine."

Trish reached her arms around the back of Wade's neck. "It just so happens that I love you too,

Wade Holbrook. But where does that leave us? I'm supposed to work on Monday."

He leaned down to close the gap between their lips. "Call in sick."

Trish's heart soared, and her entire body tingled as the kiss deepened. Wade lifted her off her feet as the rain poured around them.

"Please say you'll stay in Starlight," Wade whispered, his breath hot against her ear. "Think of all the books you could write."

"But I haven't even published one yet."

Wade flashed her his charming smile that always made her come unglued. "But you will. I believe in you."

Trish ignored the horns honking all around them, and kissed him again.

 **rish**

FOUR MONTHS LATER . . .

"YOU LOOK AMAZING!" Mindy squealed at the sight of Trish in the dress she'd picked up at Betsy's Boot Boutique earlier that day. One that paired quite well with her newest pair of boots. Trish was sure she might have a problem, now that she owned three pairs of cowgirl boots. But she wore them everywhere.

"You don't think it's too much?"

"Honey, you're the guest of honor! This party is going to blow my last one out of the water!"

Trish's life still didn't seem real.

She'd officially moved to Starlight a month ago. Kate used her real estate connections to help her find a cute little rental home in town. One that included a cozy writing loft on its second floor with an amazing view of the Bighorn mountains. She spent her days working at Mabel's waiting tables, her afternoons writing, and her evenings out at the ranch with Wade and Lina.

And she finally had her first published novel to show for it all.

Though she'd sent her first few chapters to Taylor, the literary agent, Trish ultimately decided to publish her first novel herself, guided by Glenda's expertise and wonderful team. Taylor had signed her on as a client, too, eager to represent her in any future opportunities that arose. Things like foreign rights, audio rights, and movie rights made Trish dizzy.

"Ready to go downstairs?"

Trish hugged Mindy tight. "I'm so happy you could be here for this. I've missed you so much. I hope you can stay for a few days?"

"That I can. I've already talked to Lina about her computer situation. If she wants to host romance writers on a regular basis, she needs to consider some upgrades. Plus, there seem to be some single cowboys lurking around."

A tiny bubble of hope formed that her best

friend might find a reason to move to Starlight too, but Trish didn't say so out loud.

Trish had been cooped up in the guest room upstairs most of the afternoon, completely unaware of the preparations happening downstairs. But one look into the living room below, and Trish's eyes teared up.

A big banner hung across the fireplace mantel, reading *Congratulations! You're now a published author!* A table beneath the big bay window was filled with paperback copies of her book *Starlight Nights.* Wade stood at the foot of the stairs, waiting to take her arm. He beamed up at her with such love in his eyes that she nearly melted into a puddle on her descent.

"I'm so proud of you," he whispered against her ear before placing a kiss at the base of her neck. Shivers coursed through her. Would Wade always make her feel this way with the softest touch?

The living room was filled with more people than Trish realized she knew: Lina, Allen, Chet, Kate, Ty, little Eli. But most surprisingly, all of her writer friends were in attendance too. Glenda wrapped her in a hug just as the others joined in, making it a group affair.

"We're so stinking proud of you!" Marti said with an additional squeeze.

"I can't believe you guys all made it!"

"You kidding?" Glenda said. "We wouldn't have missed this for the world."

"Can I have your attention please?" Wade called from the center of the room. He waited until a hush fell over the room. Trish felt her cheeks blaze a bit red, but she met his eyes and felt her fraying nerves at the overabundant attention calm. "I just want to say a few words about our amazing guest of honor. Trish Meadows, would you come here please?"

She sheepishly made her way across the room, stopping when she was hardly a foot in front of Wade. Her heart rate jumped at the fiery look in his eyes. The room around them disappeared for a moment, lost in his gaze that she was.

"I was determined to spend my life alone, too afraid to take a chance on something real. But you showed me that some risks are worth taking. I'm so incredibly proud of you for chasing your dream. I'm thankful you chose to stay in Starlight, and even more thankful that you chose to put up with me."

An audience of laughter surrounded them at that comment.

"I love you more every day. Would you give me just one more thing to be thankful for?" He bent on one knee and presented a small blue velvet box. "Would you do me the honor of becoming my wife?"

The room erupted in gasps, quieting as they eagerly awaited an answer.

Tears beaded at the corners of her eyes. "Of course I will."

Cheers and a few whistles sounded. Shadow added a few barks of approval. Wade slipped a beautiful ring onto her finger and drew her in for a toe-curling kiss. Between the man she loved and his wonderful family, Trish finally had her own happily ever after.

THE END

Please consider leaving an honest review online. Reviews help readers find new books to love. I read and appreciate each review!

Sign up for Jacqueline Winter's newsletter to receive alerts about current projects and new releases!

http://eepurl.com/du18iz

ACKNOWLEDGMENTS

To my Family - Thank you all for the unyielding support, and thank you most of all for believing in me and this crazy dream of mine.

To my Critique Team - Thank you for your flexibility, your honest feedback, and most of all your time. This story would not have become what it did without you.

To my Editorial Team - Thank you for helping me to shape my story into a shiny work of art I can be sincerely proud of. I appreciate each of you beyond words.

To my Cover Artist - Thank you for creating such a beautiful cover I cannot stop staring at. It genuinely captures the essence of the story.

To my Readers - Thank you for reading my stories. Thank you for your kind reviews and encouraging words. They truly make my day and are the reason I know I've set out on the right path.

To my Dog - Thank you for your unconditional love and putting up with my long writing nights. I promise many long walks and adventures to come.

ABOUT THE AUTHOR

Jacqueline Winters has been writing since she was nine when she'd sneak stacks of paper from her grandma's closet and fill them with adventure. She grew up in small-town Nebraska and spent a decade living in beautiful Alaska. She writes sweet contemporary romance and contemporary romantic suspense.

She's a sucker for happily ever afters, has a sweet tooth that can be sated with cupcakes, and believes sangria was possibly the best invention ever. On a relaxing evening, you can find her at her computer writing her next novel with her faithful dog poking his adorable head out from beneath her desk.

facebook.com/JacquelineWintersRomance

goodreads.com/jacquelinewinters

www.ingramcontent.com/pod-product-compliance
Lightning Source LLC
Chambersburg PA
CBHW020759250626
47155CB00003B/1146